HEARTBEAT

THE REAL LIFE STORY

HEARTBEAT

THE REAL LIFE STORY

HILARY BONNER

YORKSHIRE
TELEVISION

BOXTREE

First published in Great Britain in 1994 by
Boxtree Limited

1 3 5 7 9 10 8 6 4 2

Designed by Maggie Aldred
Typeset by SX Composing
Printed and bound in Portugal by Printer Portuguesa

Boxtree Limited
Broadwall House
21 Broadwall
London SE1 9PL

A CIP catalogue entry for this book is available from the
British Library.

ISBN 1 85283 474 9

Jacket photographs courtesy of Yorkshire Television

Additional material on Nick Berry courtesy of Daisy Alexandra

Contents

Acknowledgements   6

Chapter 1   7
THE HISTORY OF *HEARTBEAT*
Heartbeat's Characters   14

Chapter 2   20
NICK BERRY (NICK ROWAN)

Chapter 3   30
NIAMH CUSACK (KATE ROWAN)

Chapter 4   39
AIDENSFIELD FOLK: THE REGULARS

Chapter 5   55
AT THE STATION

Chapter 6   65
THE SIXTIES LOOK OF *HEARTBEAT*

Chapter 7   78
BEHIND THE SCENES: ON LOCATION

Chapter 8   89
HEATBEAT: CHAPTER AND VERSE
The Sixties Sound of *Heartbeat*   89

Cast List   124

ACKNOWLEDGEMENTS

The author and publishers would like to thank the *Heartbeat* team: notably Keith Richardson, Steve Lanning, Martin Auty, Pat Brown, Teresa Ferlinc – who was never too busy to answer endless queries, Susie Tullett and Clare de Vries. In addition, from Yorkshire Television: Sheila Fitzhugh and Andrea Pitchforth of the Stills Department for their invaluable help with pictures, Jacqui Williams, Alex Bailey, the photographer on series two, three and four of *Heartbeat*, and David Eaton for additional pictures.

CHAPTER

1

THE HISTORY OF
HEARTBEAT

—

Heartbeat has been one of the most successful ITV drama series of the last twenty years. The exploits of its country policeman hero and his doctor wife now pull in up to 17 million viewers an episode, and regularly challenge *Coronation Street* in the weekly ratings war.

Heartbeat is a record breaker. By the end of 1994 programme-makers Yorkshire TV predict that twenty-five countries worldwide will be plugged into this unlikely blockbuster. If Yorkshire could package the formula of *Heartbeat's* success and sell it they would make a fortune. In the cut-throat world of big-time television this is a property to die for.

Set in the Sixties, *Heartbeat's* gentle nostalgia has proven quite irresistible. Its leading actors, Nick Berry and Niamh Cusack, have become television superstars – so much so that Yorkshire TV have signed Nick up on a golden-handcuffs contract. He is the wonder boy of the moment and they have no intention of losing him. 'I think viewers want to watch people on screen they can like, and enjoy looking back on the past, particularly a time like the Sixties which they remember as being much more pleasant and fun than now', says Nick Berry. '*Heartbeat* is all about "the good old days" – which probably never existed, but it's nice to think they did.'

Whatever the secret, *Heartbeat* was a winner from the beginning, yet its story is a fascinating one. For a start this huge hit of a programme was one that nearly

▲ PC Nick Rowan (Nick Berry) and his doctor wife, Kate (Niamh Cusack), soon after their arrival in Aidensfield.

got away – *Heartbeat* was on and off the drawing-board for so long it seemed unlikely it would ever be made.

It all began fifteen years ago when Yorkshire TV bought the rights to a little-known series of books written by a country policeman under the pen-name of Nicholas Rhea. The Leeds-based company wanted to make a major drama series set in their own area, and Rhea's novels – the first was called *Constable on the Hill* – featured a young village policeman stationed in the heart of the Yorkshire Moors.

'We had just finished *Yellow Thread Street* in Hong Kong (in 1990) and we felt we were neglecting our own doorstep', says Yorkshire's head of drama and *Heartbeat* executive producer, Keith Richardson. 'Somebody came in with the *Constable* books and they seemed just what we were looking for.'

The author of the books, a serving police officer whose real name was Peter Walker, was ecstatic. 'I thought I had struck gold', he remembers. 'I thought that was it. I went to meetings at Yorkshire and talked about it and assumed that a TV series was about to be made.'

But it never happened. And nobody can quite remember why. Says Keith: 'It was just one of those projects that never quite got off the ground. One factor was certainly the success of *All Creatures Great and Small*, which was very big at the time and in many ways was the same kind of show and also set in the same part of Yorkshire.'

Yorkshire TV continued to pay an annual sum for the rights to the *Constable* books for three years. Then they abandoned the project. Peter Walker, Yorkshire born and bred and still living in the county, vividly recalls his feelings at the time: 'I was terribly disappointed, of course, but I had friends who were writers who explained to me that this often happens.'

Walker, who had retired from the police force as an inspector in charge of public relations, got on with his life and his writing. He has now published a staggering eighty-one books under his own name and various pseudonyms, including fourteen *Constable* books and one volume of novelizations of *Heartbeat*.

Yorkshire took up a second option on the books in 1988 and decided they wanted to make some changes before actually producing the first *Heartbeat* series in 1990. In the original books PC Nick Rowan is a young married man just as we see him on TV – but his wife, Mary, is a traditional police wife who does not work but devotes her life to looking after her children and backing up her husband. Yorkshire TV decided they needed an extra element to turn the *Constable* books into a winner on the box, so they sat down and coolly calculated exactly what ingredients were guaranteed to bring in the viewers.

Yorkshire already had the huge hit *Darling Buds of May*. They wanted to continue to succeed on that level, and they wanted to create another, younger star who would aspire to the heights of popularity achieved by David Jason. The programme makers began to believe that with one or two amendments these homely tales of the life of a village bobby could do just that.

▶ *The man who made it happen: Yorkshire TV's Head of Drama and* Heartbeat *executive producer, Keith Richardson.*

◀ Our heroes:
Kate Rowan – the complete country doctor;
▶ Nick Rowan – the perfect village bobby.

The period was right. TV bosses are well aware that in the harsh, recession-hit Nineties people are looking back at the past through distinctly rose-coloured spectacles – and they can't get enough of it. Sixties nostalgia was already big business on screen and in the record shops. The spirit of the *Constable* books was also right. Gentle TV is the flavour of the moment – people have enough grim realism on the violent streets of modern Britain – and the viewer appeal of police stories was already well proven.

'So to get that bit extra, we started to think of what else always attracted huge audiences', explains Keith Richardson. 'The answer was obvious. Anything to do with hospitals and medicine. We decided we would give our bobby a doctor wife. That would add to the programme's appeal and give us the whole new element we were looking for. Then we started to think about a title and between us came up with *Heartbeat* – the heart represented the medical side and the beat was the policemen's beat.'

Keith and his team, with the help of casting directors, began to look for the stars of their show. They wanted a young man with charisma who was already a name – someone to carry the show. Nick Berry, a TV favourite through *EastEnders*, was always a likely candidate.

'From the moment I met Nick Berry I knew he was the one', says Richardson.

'It was the same with Niamh Cusack. They were good together from the start too. They look right as a couple and there is a spark between them. And once we had got those two right the rest just carried on.'

Somebody remembered there was a Buddy Holly hit called 'Heartbeat' and that seemed the perfect theme song. Because Nick Berry already had a bit of a recording career behind him he was asked to rerecord the song. Yet there was at first no plan to make a big deal out of Sixties music. The sound of *Heartbeat*, which has given the series such a distinctive flavour and is now widely credited with much of its popularity, happened completely by accident.

'It was a chance thing which developed during the filming of the first series', remembers Keith. 'We had people listening to radios in their kitchens and of course the radios had to be playing Sixties music. Gradually we started to use more and more of the music and then it sort of spilled over so that by the time the series went out we had Sixties music dubbed into all kinds of scenes. And of course it has become one of the most distinctive aspects of the series. But in the beginning it wasn't deliberate at all.'

The first series of *Heartbeat* was produced by ex-*Emmerdale* boss Stuart Doughty. He and his team centred the drama around the unspoiled moorland village of Goathland, which became the fictional Aidensfield. From the start the stunning scenery of the North Yorks Moors was to play its own starring role in *Heartbeat*.

The visual side of the show and its homely village life background have remained a constant factor. But when Steve Lanning, a man with more of a film background, took over as producer in the second series he began to toughen up *Heartbeat*. 'We decided we wanted to make it a little less cosy and have harder storylines', he said. 'Certainly the format works a treat.'

Steve handed over the fourth series to Yorkshire-born producer Martyn Auty. More than a dozen directors have worked on the forty-five episodes so far filmed, but the crew, including lighting cameramen Dave Steadman and Peter Hardman and sound supervisor Paul Venner, have remained virtually unchanged from the start.

Guest stars are a big part of *Heartbeat*. A fascinating and impressive number of performers have appeared alongside Nick and Niamh, including: Jean Anderson (*Coronation Street*'s Hilda Ogden), Annette Crosbie, Eleanor Bron, Peter Barkworth, Dorothy Tutin, comedian Duggie Brown, Dora Bryan, Nick's real-life girlfriend Rachel Robertson, Freddie Garrity (of the Sixties pop group Freddie and the Dreamers), Julie T. Wallace, Anne Stallybrass, Phyllida Law and Tim Healy.

Countries which now show *Heartbeat* include Australia, where the show is as popular as it is in Britain, Bulgaria, Canada, Cyprus, Iceland, Ireland, Israel, Kenya, Lithuania, New Zealand, Romania, Saudi Arabia, Slovenia, South Africa and Zimbabwe.

Says Yorkshire TV's international sales director Sue Crawley: '*Heartbeat* is eminently saleable. Every week we are doing new deals. We quite expect to have

▲ Nick chats to Steve Lanning, producer of Series 2 and 3.

sold to at least twenty-five countries by the end of 1994 and we are very optimistic about doing a deal in America, which is always the hard one to crack. *Heartbeat* is timeless. It doesn't date. It is a very nice little earner on the international market and that means we are generating funds to make more episodes.'

The series now bears little resemblance to Peter Walker's original books. The stories are completely new and written by a team of scriptwriters. The first series did use storylines from the books, but after that there was not enough material and in any case Yorkshire's decision to toughen up *Heartbeat* called for harder-hitting storylines than any that appeared in the *Constable* books.

Peter Walker is not offended. 'I think it is always true that TV series and films go away from the original books', he says. 'But they have kept many of my characters, which I like.' Sergeant Blaketon and PC Ventress are both Peter Walker inventions, but not PC Bellamy – he was introduced to keep the show young. Greengrass is also in the original books.

The characters of *Heartbeat* are now firmly established in television folklore. Indeed Nick, Kate, the people of Aidensfield and the staff of Ashfordly police station all have their own histories carefully documented by Yorkshire TV; and it is their backgrounds that have made them into the characters we now see on screen.

HEARTBEAT'S CHARACTERS

—

PC Nick Rowan

Nick was born in London in 1938 and joined the Met after a somewhat rebellious youth. He met and married Kate in 1961 when he was working in central London and she was a young doctor training at a large teaching hospital. As a result of his own experience Nick wants to be a kindly copper in the *Dixon of Dock Green* mould. He is firmly committed to the ideal of community policing – a concept which he saw being eroded in London during the early Sixties by social change and new attitudes.

He had been evacuated to the North Yorks Moors as a boy during the war and childhood memories combined with the link with Kate meant that when he decided he wanted to quit the big city, Yorkshire immediately appealed.

Nick hopes that by becoming a village bobby he will be able to work with people rather than crime statistics. In Aidensfield he finds the independence he craves and is free to contribute to community life.

Dr Kate Rowan

Kate is intelligent, middle class and a very caring doctor. She viewed the move northwards with mixed feelings. She was born not far from Aidensfield and when she won a place at London University to study medicine she felt in some ways that she had escaped from her native Yorkshire. From the beginning, medical life thrilled her. She had a job in one of the most technologically advanced hospitals in the country, and so was dubious when Nick suggested leaving London. However, she decided it was a time when her husband's career came first, and she was aware that the long hours demanded by hospital work were putting a strain on their marriage.

She hoped that she might work for her childhood mentor, Aidensfield's ageing GP Alex Ferrenby. But Ferrenby at first believed Aidensfield was not ready for a woman doctor, who would not be physically or mentally strong enough for a country practice. Kate resented his prejudice, considered having a child and settling down as a housewife, but ultimately fought back.

Claude Jeremiah Greengrass

Greengrass is a likeable but totally untrustworthy rogue with an eye for the main chance. As a criminal he is very minor league – poaching, handling stolen goods, and so forth. He has no regular job though he does live on a scruffy

small-holding which is the nearest thing he has to a front for his more dubious activities. Nick appreciates him as a local character but also finds him a pain in the neck and usually deals with him by handing out rough justice rather than sticking to the letter of the law. Greengrass's fortunes change with the weather. A great deal of money earned through a nefarious land deal turns overnight into a tax bill leaving him broke and in debt. But you know he will get by. He is an old-fashioned country man, deeply attached to his flea-bitten lurcher, Alfred.

▲ *The look of love: Nick and Kate in a rare moment of off-duty togetherness.*

Sergeant Oscar Blaketon

Blaketon is section head of Ashfordly police station, and as such Nick's immediate superior. Punctilious, pedantic and bureaucratic, Blaketon sees his job as enforcing the law without holding any opinions on it. He is, however, a supremely professional officer, and his unyielding exterior hides a surprisingly soft heart. He also has considerable insight into human nature and the character of the community. His weakness is his obsession with Greengrass; his determination to see the man convicted of almost anything can sometimes cloud his judgement.

▶ *Claude
Jeremiah
Greengrass (Bill
Maynard) up to no
good, as usual.*

Blaketon is divorced. His marriage broke up because of the long hours involved in police work. His ex-wife and eighteen-year-old son Graham live some way away in Pickering, and for most of the boy's childhood the only chance Blaketon has had to see his son has been at school football matches.

He is a religious man, a Methodist, and loves the big-band music of Glenn Miller.

▲ Sergeant Blaketon (Derek Fowlds) gives Nick one of his looks . . .

PC Alf Ventress

PC Alf Ventress is not a Sixties man. Alf likes his food and enjoys a smoke – hence his nickname, the Human Ashtray. With his uniform straining at the seams, Alf lumbers through life determined to keep his head down and any excessive activity at bay.

Ventress is not the high flier of the North Riding Police and is simply content to wait for retirement, but since he has been at Ashfordly police station longer than anyone else, he can instantly lay hands on any particular file. He also has a remarkable memory for local characters, gossip and incidents, however long ago. There is a Mrs Ventress somewhere in the background who packs his lunchtime sandwiches – but we never see her.

PC Phil Bellamy

Young Bellamy is a bit of a Jack-the-lad, a naughty nice guy – though always pleasant and helpful. Things have been looking up for Bellamy since the arrival of Nick Rowan at Ashfordly police station. He has been gradually transformed from a bored time-server – who was initially attracted to the job as a means of steady income and getting a bit of status – to a young man with ambition. In Nick, he has found someone nearer his own age who is keen and interested, and Nick's enthusiasm begins to rub off on Bellamy – he has even started to do a lot more studying.

He has a relentlessly complicated love-life which gets him in to all manner of scrapes. He is an athletic chap, a keen footballer, and quite useful to Nick if he gets involved in any rough stuff.

George Ward

George is the landlord of The Aidensfield Arms. Despite his occasionally surly disposition, he warmed to Nick earlier than most of the villagers, and sometimes passes on helpful tips gleaned from pub gossip – about poaching, for instance. He has the landlord's natural tendency to run with the hare and hunt with the hounds, but George has at times stood up for what he thinks is right. He once came to Kate's rescue when she was dangerously confronted by a small mob. Kate diagnosed him as suffering from a rare disease of the immune system, myasthenia gravis, which means he tires easily. This illness, however, is controlled by regular medication.

Gina Ward

Gina is George's niece. Because of his medical condition George needs help running the pub and Gina arrives from Liverpool in her bubble-car at just the right moment. In fact she only came to Aidensfield because it was a condition of her probation. Following a tempestuous few years at home, culminating in a conviction for handling stolen goods – with a suspicion that many other offences should have been taken into consideration – the legal system of Liverpool just wanted to be rid of her. She avoided a prison sentence on condition that she should be sent out of temptation to work for her uncle in the country.

She is eighteen, extremely fashion conscious, and well able to take care of herself. She terrifies the life out of some of the pub's regulars.

Dr James Radcliffe

Radcliffe becomes a major character in the fourth series of *Heartbeat*. He is a GP with a practice in Whitby, who has invited Kate to join him as a partner while accepting that she will also remain Aidensfield's village doctor. Radcliffe's wife died two years earlier, leaving him with two young daughters to look after.

He has a devoted receptionist, Christine, who looks after the day-to-day running of the practice and is only too eager to help him look after the children whenever he wants.

▼ *Gina (Tricia Penrose), the barmaid: George's niece and bad-girl-turned-good.*

▲ *George Ward (Stuart Golland), the landlord of the Aidensfield Arms.*

2

NICK BERRY
(Nick Rowan)

—

Nick Berry has reached whole new heights of stardom as PC Nick Rowan – and he is not giving it up. The actor who made his name in *EastEnders* will stay in the top TV role for as long as the writers keep coming up with the ideas and Yorkshire TV are prepared to make the hit series.

'There is no question of my quitting,' he says. 'Those stories are all absolute nonsense. I am very happy in this role.'

Nick knows that he is on to a very good thing indeed. 'I am aware of how *Heartbeat* has changed my life. Suddenly, I seem to have this high profile and I never fail to be surprised at the kind of offers that are coming in now. Before, I was just a jobbing actor going from audition to audition, and now I'm getting offered stuff.'

Nick is honest enough to admit that there is another attraction of being the leading man in the most successful drama series on TV.

'Since I play the central character in *Heartbeat,* things are inclined to revolve around me. That makes you quite important, I'm afraid. The whole business is now so star-driven – whatever the project, they want to know who is going to be in it.

So I get pampered and looked after which is lovely. *EastEnders* was a company show, it wasn't like that at all. Everybody mucks in, that is the way it works.

Here, I get all this fuss made of me – if I have a headache or a cold every-

body rushes around looking after me. It's logical because if I go sick it disrupts the whole show. I have a driver and a car and all those things. It's like being a child. It's wonderful.'

Nick, 30, flashes that grin which has brought him such a huge female following. He is an extremely good-looking young man, and Yorkshire TV have been quick to spot that his 1990s-style matinée idol looks could become quite priceless.

Yet his joy in the way of life his success has brought him remains almost child-like. 'I'm in a very privileged situation, what else can I do but enjoy it?' he asks, although he feels that perhaps he shouldn't admit to enjoying it so much. 'It's not that I am in the business for all of that,' he points out quickly. 'It's just one of the things that I find extraordinary. And it is good to go home at the weekend to re-adjust yourself.'

Home is a town house in Islington, North London, which he shares with

▲ *Straight to camera: Nick Berry as PC Nick Rowan.*

21

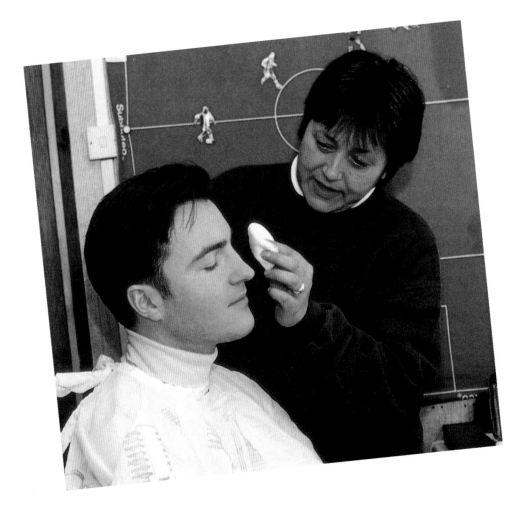

▲ *The finishing touches: Nick with make-up supervisor, Jill Rogerson.*

actress-girlfriend Rachel Robertson.

Rachel appeared in the second series of *Heartbeat* ('Wall of Silence') as a teenage girl who aborted her brother's child. Incest and its grizzly results were a powerful subject for a show like *Heartbeat* and at the last moment producer Steve Lanning decided to cut some of the more controversial scenes.

Nick had lived in Islington for almost nine years, in a flat before buying his house. It's an area of London he is fond of and does not plan to leave although he admits that he would also like to have a place in the country. 'Maybe if I do a few more series of *Heartbeat* I'll get the country place,' he says. 'It would be nice to have somewhere bigger.'

Nick is fiercely protective about his personal life, and as his popularity increases, his home becomes even more of a haven and one of the few places he can enjoy normal peace and quiet.

Filming *Heartbeat* does mean he leads a kind of double life. Mornings in Yorkshire start at around 6 am, and the first port of call is the make-up bus. After the daily routine of hair slicking and shaving, Nick sits down to breakfast – a mug of tea and a couple of slices of toast – while he studies his scenes for the

▲ Nick looks over the script with producer Martyn Auty, director Tim Dowd and executive producer Keith Richardson.

▶ Night rider: PC Rowan on the Frances Barnet motorbike which was acquired for the series.

day ahead. The peace and tranquility of moorland mornings makes it his favourite time, although he finds it much easier to get out of bed in June than in January!

The early subdued atmosphere is broken by the noisy clamour of a film crew in action erecting the light and sound equipment at the particular location of the day. By 8.30 am filming is underway. After a day's work Nick likes to relax quietly to prepare for tomorrow. 'Very often I have a drink with the crew, wander home to my bed, and gaze out of the window into the night sky pondering what the weather has in store . . .'

In London his days start art around 8.30 am. First there is some gentle exercise with TV's Mr Motivator, then the same kind of breakfast he eats on set, and then a mail-answering session. Yet he says: 'I'm not terribly organized, and sometimes mail lies around unanswered for a while. I have the best intentions, but not the time to achieve all the goals I set myself in a weekend. That's what I enjoy about *Heartbeat* and Yorkshire. Everyone is sensitive to my workload and commitments and so I am protected from myself.'

Apart from Rachel, there is only one thing about London life which Nick misses when he is up in Yorkshire. 'West Ham,' he says, immediately. A born and bred Londoner, he is a devoted West Ham fan. There are few videos of *Heartbeat* or *EastEnders* to be found in his home; instead the walls are lined with shelves of video tapes of West Ham games and other big matches. Ask him if he would have liked to have been anything other than an actor and there can only be one answer. 'A footballer,' he says with a grin. 'If I could be anyone in the world at any time in history, I would choose to be Bobby Moore lifting the World Cup in 1966.'

He has become greatly influenced by *Heartbeat*, not only by the countryside in which it is set, but also by the Sixties period which dominates it. 'I really locked into the period years ago, and *Heartbeat* has indulged me completely with that great sense of style,' he says. He also loves many of the Sixties pop artists whose music is played on the show, like the Searchers, Herman's Hermits, and the Everly Brothers.

When it comes to cars, Nick owns an E-Type Jaguar which is also of the right period. 'It's ironic that it is a Sixties car,' he says. 'I wanted one from when I was a little boy, E-Types were absolutely my dream car.

Predictably, therefore, Nick adores the old MG which, as Nick Rowan, he has been rebuilding in *Heartbeat*: 'It's gorgeous, really lovely.'

Nick has only one misgiving about *Heartbeat*: 'I think Nick Rowan is a bit too successful! He is still a regular PC and yet he solves every crime; and he is at an age where he should be promoted. I am hoping that the series will start to touch on his lack of ambition. He really is more than happy and fulfilled as a village bobby. He loves the countryside. He loves the people and the lifestyle. His wife is the quietly ambitious one. And now, in terms of exploring their relationship, a little bit more friction develops in the fourth series.

'The show has to change. The stories have become harder-nosed as the series

◀ *Nick Rowan at the wheel of his beloved MG which he painstakingly rebuilt.*

▲ On the beat.

◀ Both Nick Berry and Niamh Cusack fell for the stunning landscape of the Yorkshire Moors while filming Heartbeat.

▲ *Nick with the
production team,
in preparation for
the next scene.*

has gone on. We started off with cats being stuck up trees and that was a big drama. We have moved on to a lot more heavy issues. I think you learn as a series like this grows what is right for it and what is not. Nick Rowan has this perfect, charmed life. He wakes up in the morning to a bright, loving wife, opens the door to a picturesque vista, spends the day solving crimes, avoiding Blaketon, laughing at Greengrass, comes home for his tea and then goes to the pub. It's all perfect!' Nick did not even dream that *Heartbeat* would be such a big hit. 'I must admit that with the first series of *Heartbeat* I felt that its success was a bit of a fluke,' he says. 'I certainly didn't think that it would take off in the way that it did.' He became more impressed as the storylines became harder.

Nick may have fallen in love with the wilder parts of Yorkshire while filming *Heartbeat*, but he remains a dedicated Londoner. He went to Aldersbrook Primary School in Manor Park, and that was where he developed a taste for acting. 'I can remember the first time I was on stage,' he says. 'I played one of the Three Wise Men in the school nativity play.

'There were a group of us at school who all started acting at the same time. When I was about seven or eight, one of the mums at school organized this old-time music-hall show to raise money for charity at the Stratford Theatre Royal. We went round performing in old people's homes and hospitals. Then the same mum, Sylvia Young, set up an agency and I started doing commercials. It was all pure fluke. If I hadn't gone into it then I don't think I would have had an acting career.'

Wherever he goes, Nick finds recognition nowadays. He is a young man with a bright future, but right now he is quite content to stick with PC Nick Rowan and *Heartbeat*.

▲ Nick relaxes off set and takes advantage of being in the countryside . . .

▶ . . . and an informal moment between filming sessions.

3

NIAMH CUSACK
(Kate Rowan)

—

Niamh has won the hearts of millions as Dr Kate Rowan. She has an outstanding acting pedigree as a scion of one of the most famous acting families in the business – but she was nearly the one that got away. The daughter of legendary Cyril Cusack, and sister of actresses Sinead and Sorcha and later Catherine, Niamh first trained to be a flautist. She was also married to a musician, cellist Roland Saggs. They met at the Royal College of Music in London and then worked together in Dublin.

It was after they decided to return to England that Niamh decided she was in the wrong job: 'We had absolutely nothing, we hadn't a bean, and we were renting a room in a house in Thornton Heath. We were both practising away and I was on a scholarship and I had some money to study as well, but without playing in an orchestra, without the sort of social side, the performing side, I was acutely aware of how much I really didn't enjoy playing the flute. Being with someone who so completely enjoyed playing the cello made me even more aware of it.

'We had talked about whether I would go to university, and I decided one Saturday to go into the City Lit in Covent Garden and sign up for some French classes and maybe take A-level French because I had only done Irish exams and I wasn't sure these would get me into an English university. They had drama classes on the same day. I thought that I would just pop in and see what the people

◀ *Niamh, as Dr Kate Rowan, in the fur-lined duffel coat specially designed to keep her warm in Heartbeat*

▼ *and during a scene in the surgery.*

giving these classes were like. And I signed up for a Saturday class.

'I came home on the first evening after drama class, and I was on air. I just knew. I thought this is it. This is me. Why didn't I think of this before? They turned out to be really brilliant classes and a lot of people going to them began applying for drama school. So, like the sheep I was, I did as well, and I got into the Guildhall School of Music and Drama and did a year there.

'I became very determined. In my first term I went to the Royal Exchange Theatre in Manchester and said: "You have got to see me." I was suddenly taken over by this forceful self-confident new personality which was: "I am amazing and you must meet me." I never had it before and I actually lost it very soon afterwards – but it worked. I think you have to be like that in the beginning.

'When you have had a career which hasn't worked out you sort of feel, well, what have I got to lose?'

One of the most daunting aspects of Niamh's career change was having to tell her father that she planned to follow in his famous footsteps. He was supportive but had strong reservations. 'He thought I was too softly spoken. He didn't think anybody would hear me past the first two rows. I told the director of my first big stage play this when he gave me the part of Desdemona in *Othello*. He said: "Well, let's give him a seat in the third row, then."

'I wouldn't have described myself even then as soft-spoken, but I did work at my voice, and I think I have learned a lot. I had a wonderful voice teacher at the Guildhall called Patsy Rothenberg, who is now a voice coach at the National Theatre. Lots of actors go to her including Richard Wilson from *One Foot In The Grave*. You do feel yourself getting better.'

The different paths Niamh and Roland were now following and the separations caused by their work took their toll and eventually they divorced.

Niamh met the present man in her life, Irish actor Barry Lynch, when she appeared on stage in Dublin with her elder sisters Sinead and Sorcha in Chekhov's *Three Sisters*, in which Barry played the part of soldier baron Tusenbach. It was an extraordinary family production, which also starred Cyril Cusack and was, by Niamh's own admission, a momentous time in her acting career.

Niamh grew up in Ireland, and, in spite of a great closeness with her father which developed later in life, was brought up mainly by her mother.

'My parents separated when I was very young', she recalls. 'I do not remember it well. My father was still around quite a lot, and even when my parents were together he had often been away because of his work and I don't think I ever expected him to be there very much.

'I think when you are a kid you get used to things very quickly and accept the way things are. If I had been thirteen or fourteen or something it may have been more difficult; at seven or eight as long as there is food on the table and somebody to care for you I don't think there are the same problems. Also, our mum was fantastic. She was terribly strong. And I think that if that is all you know it is OK.'

In spite of her parents' reluctance for her to enter the family business, and her later decision to embark upon a musical career, Niamh did have one foray as a child actor.

'There was a film called *Where's Jack?* with Tommy Steele where the director was a friend of my father's. He came to our house and asked me if I would like to be in his film. I said yes, and then he asked me how much I would like to be paid. I said £50, which for me was like billions of pounds, and he said all right.

'But then after one day's work I got flu and that was the end of it. I do appear, I am in, but only just, and I don't speak. I was supposed to say something but the flu put a stop to that. None the less, and I still remember this, after just one day someone on the set said: "Well, she's a natural." And I think it went straight to my head. But I didn't do anything afterwards, because strangely enough considering how things have turned out, my parents didn't want any of us to be actors. They didn't want that kind of life for us.'

In adulthood Niamh and her father became great friends, and his death in October 1993 from motor neurone disease was a bitter blow. 'I don't think you ever get over losing your parents', Niamh says. 'My father was a very strong personality and it is difficult to think he will not be there any more.'

Most of Niamh's acting work has been in theatre and before *Heartbeat* her

▲ *Niamh and Nick get together to sort out a problem – their working relationship is first class.*

only television had been guest appearances in drama series like *Poirot*. She is a classically trained actress used to the luxury of carefully structured rehearsal time, and the prospect of a long-running series was a daunting one.

'I found it very hard', she admits. 'I found the swiftness of putting it together with little or no rehearsal very difficult to cope with. The four or five weeks of rehearsal you get in a play is time when you are able to get lots of different dimensions to a part and there are things you don't even know you've got in there just because you've lived with it for four weeks.'

Nick, with his *EastEnders* experience, had the edge over Niamh in the beginning. 'He took to it like a duck to water', says Niamh. 'He was really on top of it from the very beginning.'

Theirs is a relationship founded on mutual admiration and liking. 'Nick and I have a great relationship', she says. 'I think he is a natural. And I think we do manage to have a pretty kind of bubbly relationship on screen. It's lively and there is energy in it. That's to do with work and effort.'

Nevertheless, it is true to say that Nick and Niamh have little in common and are totally different kinds of actors. Niamh takes her work and her life pretty seriously. She really studies every aspect of every scene. 'Nick thinks I am far too intense because I am apt to go on and on about a scene', she says.

But Niamh is inclined to be thoughtful about *everything* that she does. Before taking on her *Heartbeat* role as a doctor, Niamh researched thoroughly. She spent a great deal of time picking the brains of real-life doctors who were GPs during the Sixties. She believes actors must learn from all that is around them.

'When I was a musician I rather wafted around the place and lived entirely in my own world', she says. 'Things happened to me rather than the other way around, and sometimes I barely noticed what was happening around me at all. Since becoming an actor I find that people kind of come at me in different colours, and I do draw on real-life people all the time for my acting.' According to Niamh, this is very much an Irish characteristic to be curious about other people and to want to delve deeper.

Nick has an altogether lighter approach, and his passion for football is every bit as important to him as his acting career. Yet in spite of their differences, Niamh is quite right: there *is* a definite spark between them on screen.

'The chemistry has to be right between these two and we think it is', says Keith Richardson. 'I knew as soon as I met Niamh that we had found Kate Rowan.'

The character of Kate has developed around Niamh – sometimes accidentally. One of the best-kept secrets of *Heartbeat* is what Niamh Cusack is wearing on her feet whenever they are out of shot. 'It will be thick woolly socks with wellies or Timberland boots, and quite probably both together', confesses Niamh. She feels the cold badly and as *Heartbeat* is shot on the chilly heights of the Yorkshire Moors and often in deepest winter, Niamh really suffers – and her wardrobe has been partly governed by her suffering.

'I feel the cold so badly I have been known to cry with it', says Niamh. 'It really can be that painful. My feet and hands are the worst, particularly my feet. And

The changing face of Dr Kate: ◀ as she was with the elaborate, authentic Sixties look in Series 1, ▲ and as she is now, sporting a more simple bob.

Sixties shoes were so much fashion shoes and all designed to be disposable that their soles are terribly thin. I freeze in them, and it is an extraordinary thing because we have a costume supervisor who goes around in bare feet and flip-flops while I am turning blue! I can't believe it. She has nothing on her feet while I am looking for thermal socks and plastic bags and things – and I am never without my thermal underwear.'

Dr Kate's trademark fur-lined duffel coat was specially made for Niamh because she feels the cold so acutely. It was the idea of Steve Lanning, producer of the second and third series. 'I think he got fed up with seeing the goose pimples every time I ventured outside the door', says Niamh.

It was also Steve who changed the image of Dr Kate in line with Niamh's own wishes. 'In the first series Kate had an almost beehive hairdo which was absolutely genuine, a real Sixties look, but it wasn't very flattering and I wasn't terribly happy with it. In fact a lot of the ad men and promotional people didn't like it either because they didn't think it did me any favours.

'Steve decided to change my hairstyle and make it much softer and turn it into a sort of a bob. And that is how it has stayed except that it is now a little bit longer than it was at first, which I like. Even though it is a softer, simpler sort of style I still have this thing you have to get used to in television where your hair is looked after and brushed and rearranged all the time and you look like a Timotei girl because that is the way they like it on TV. I am not used to being so coiffed. I am not a very coiffed sort of person.

'It can be quite funny though. Your hair looks constantly gorgeous on the screen – because Alison, who does my make-up, takes huge care – and then on the street nobody can believe it when you walk by with your little rats' tails. People can't believe it's the same person. I think Alison must find me a real challenge!'

Sixties fashions do not appeal to Niamh: 'I just say it was not my period. Martin gets so depressed because Sixties clothes really are not me. Actually I don't think they did a lot for anybody at the time unless you were like Jean Shrimpton or Twiggy. But they would have looked good in anything, and would probably have looked even better in something else.'

Perhaps to cheer up Martin Baugh, Niamh relents slightly when discussing her clothes for the fourth series. 'Actually I think some of my new outfits are quite nice. I have a couple of really nice jackets. Martin is great on colours and my skirts are pretty safe ones – not too clingly and not too short.'

Along with all of the cast and crew of *Heartbeat* Niamh stays in Goathland during filming. Like Nick she has also fallen for the stunningly pretty moorland village – even if it can be somewhat chilly from time to time. 'There was one wonderful week last June when it was really hot in Goathland and everybody was wandering around in shorts enjoying the sunshine. I remember it well. They all told me about it. I missed it, of course. I wasn't needed that week, and by the time I returned to Yorkshire we were back into thermal underwear again.'

Throughout filming Niamh likes to return to London as often as she can. 'It's not so much the place as the people that I miss', she says. 'I would actually prefer to live in the country in many ways.'

And Niamh dreams of one day going back to her native Ireland: 'Going full circle in your life is the natural thing to do. If you grow up in a place and your way of communicating and your way of being is dictated by where you have been brought up it always feels so good when you return.

'You go to London, and London is a very scary place where you have to learn lots of defences. If you are in my kind of job you have to be quite tough on the outside and work out some kind of defence mechanism. When you are at home you don't have to do that in the same way.'

Her career she describes as having been 'pretty jammy all along'. And she also refers to her job in *Heartbeat* in a similar fashion. 'As I like country life it is really good for me when we are in Goathland', she says. 'I just love going walking over the moors. You can go for miles and not see another living soul other than sheep!'

The continuing success of *Heartbeat* never fails to surprise her: 'I remember the first series as being quite unpublicized and low key. I thought I had a nice job being in a drama for ten episodes and that would probably be that. But the show took off on its own in a way which I don't think anybody imagined that it would.

'One of the nice things is that we have kept the same crew throughout and so even when we get together for a new series after six months away it doesn't feel as if you have been apart any more, and we were right back in the rhythm of things on the first day.'

So does the stage actress now feel comfortable in television after all?

'Well, I do in *Heartbeat*', she says. 'And as you get to know your character and other people's characters more it does become easier obviously. You kind of instinctively know how your character would react. But I suspect I would still be just as uneasy doing another different TV show.'

Niamh has very strong ideas about the kind of person Kate Rowan really is. And she has taken Yorkshire TV's background biography several stages further in her mind. 'I decided that Kate was probably an orphan, having lost her parents at about the age of eight. She then left Yorkshire to be brought up by an aunt and uncle in London. She was sent off to boarding school and became a rather lonely sort of person.'

Niamh remembers that both she and Nick Berry were uneasy at first about a marriage between a clever middle-class doctor and a humble young bobby.

'We talked it through and decided their whole relationship was based on sex', Niamh confesses. 'I worked out my own story of how Nick and Kate met and fell for each other instantly. Kate, who had already done a year at teaching hospital, lost her cat and he was the friendly policeman who came round.

'It all happened very fast. This is the Sixties remember. They end up in bed together and that's that. She loves him because he is very centred, very emotionally secure – just what she needs.'

Niamh likes the fact that sources of possible problems between Kate and Nick are sensibly explored in the series. 'Their jobs sometimes clash', she says.

37

▲ Caring Kate examines patient Clare Mercer (Anna Calder Marshall) in Series 2.

'Obviously as a doctor she is earning more than Nick and she would like to move house, but he is obliged to stay in the police house. The great thing about *Heartbeat*, though, is that these disagreements are dealt with – the sun never goes down on one of their quarrels. That's a very important ingredient in the series.'

In her breaks between series Niamh usually returns to her roots in the theatre. Like her partner, Barry Lynch, she is an RSC actor, but they have yet to appear in an RSC production together.

She is aware that virtually no amount of theatre work, however successful and prestigious, can bring with it anything like the fame and fortune which comes with just one TV series. 'Sometimes people are not quite sure where they know me from, but they are always very nice', she says.

Like the character she plays on television, Niamh is inclined to see the best in people. And like all of us she lives in an age when we really do not want to be continually reminded of the worst – which is so much the secret of *Heartbeat*'s popularity.

AIDENSFIELD FOLK:
The Regulars

—

BILL MAYNARD
(Claude Jeremiah Greengrass)

He has a reputation for being the king of the scene-stealers, and as Claude Jeremiah Greengrass, comedy veteran Bill Maynard has pulled off his master stroke.

Greengrass was destined to be just a small supporting part in *Heartbeat* – but Yorkshire TV reckoned without the determination of 65-year-old Bill, who lent his own larger-than-life personality to the character he was asked to play: 'I could see the potential in Greengrass and I set out to make him funnier.'

Bill had to make Greengrass bigger too. In the original books and the first *Heartbeat* scripts he was described as 'a skinny ferret of a man'. 'As I am six foot one and a trim twenty stone I had to fill the character out a bit', says Bill.

As well as his personality, he also lent the old rogue his clothes. In Bill's words: 'I could see in my mind exactly how he should look. His boots are mine. I was given them twenty years ago when I made the film *Hitler – My Part In His Downfall* with Spike Milligan. I bought them afterwards for £2 from wardrobe and they became my lucky boots. I wore them for *Selwyn Froggit* and *The Gaffer*. The collarless shirts are also mine.'

▲ *Bill Maynard in jovial mood as village rogue, Claude Jeremiah Greengrass.*

Greengrass's clothes – the World War Two army greatcoat was the inspired choice of Yorkshire's costume department – are as much his uniform as Nick Rowan's police gear. In the words of costume designer Martin Baugh: 'Bill is an old variety artist who knows the value of looking the same all the time. It's an art. And it works.'

Greengrass's trademark twitchy eyes are a Maynard invention. 'I got that idea from an old rascal I knew once. He would always screw up his eyes and twitch when he told lies. And as Greengrass is a devious old villain, I twitch my eyes whenever he is supposed to be lying or embarrassed.'

Bill reckons there is a special bond between Greengrass and Rowan – or 'Ronan' as Claude Jeremiah calls him. He still cannot get his name right.

'There is definitely a bond, albeit a strange one', says Bill. 'One is a rogue and the other is a copper, yet they have this thing, they are both on their own, both outsiders – Greengrass because he is the village rogue and Nick because he is from the south. So they have a sort of affinity in a way.

'Greengrass looks upon Nick entirely differently to Blaketon with whom he has always been at daggers drawn. But most people like Greengrass in spite of his faults. Even Dr Kate has a soft spot for him. There is a nice slant to him. He is on the side of the badgers and all of that. In fact he probably prefers badgers to people, really.'

Bill is an actor who likes to do things his way. When he gets into a role he always feels he knows best. 'I have been in this business a long time', he says by way of justification. However, the people he works for do not always see it that way. 'Virtually every TV company I have ever worked for has sent me packing, saying I will never work for them again', he admits. 'I usually do, though . . .' So far there have been no problems between Bill and Yorkshire TV. Just as Greengrass is accepted as a character in the village of Aidensfield, so the burly, garrulous Bill is accepted as a character on the *Heartbeat* set.

Bill's career has indeed been a long and varied one, with good times and bad both at work and at home. He was the only child of a soldier and started out as a child entertainer in the Midlands. He remembers: 'I used to do George Formby imitations on a plank laid across a couple of beer crates. By the time I was nine years old I had nine different acts, including a cowboy act, a mandolin number, an Italian monologue and a drag turn.

'That went on until I was fifteen, then I got deeply embarrassed by the idea of being an entertainer. So I went into professional football, which was fine until I pulled a ligament.

'Then I started out at Butlin's as a band singer, and in 1952 I followed Arthur English into the Windmill: five shows a day, seven days a week, for £100 – which was the highest money they had ever paid.

'After that I got a television series with Terry Scott. I was the punk of my day. Mothers would write in and complain because I wore sweaters with an open-necked shirt. It was as if I'd had a ring through my nose.

'By 1957 I was getting £1,000 a week, topping the last of the variety bills

around the country. I had kids in private school, the large house in Hampstead, the lot. Two years later I got caught for a lot of back tax and everything had to go. My wife ended up as an optician's receptionist back in the Midlands.

'But that time John Neville had taken me on at the Nottingham Playhouse, and to get the money back I remember doing matinées of *A Midsummer Night's Dream*, evenings of *Semi-Detached*, and then going around the clubs in Leeds doing my solo act amid flying beer mats. By that time I was a TV has-been, and the clubs don't let you forget that. Stars had their names written in coloured chalk on the club blackboards. Mine was always in white.

'Eventually I got so desperate that my wife and I put an ad in the *International Herald Tribune* offering to go to America as butler and cook. The day it appeared I got my first *Till Death Us Do Part* film. They even gave me my own car parking space at Shepperton studios. I didn't dare tell them I hadn't got a car, and to save the travelling costs I used to hide out in the studios at night and sleep in my dressing room.

'But then suddenly I began to get work as an actor in television. There were Dennis Potter plays and a series called *The Life of Riley* which went above *Coronation Street* in the ratings. Having lost everything once, I was careful not to do it again.'

By the early Eighties Bill was right back at the top of the showbusiness tree. His TV sit-coms *Oh No, It's Selwyn Froggit* (twenty-eight episodes) and *The Gaffer* (twenty episodes), both ratings blockbusters, made him one of the most successful character actors in the country.

41

Sadly his first wife, Muriel, died of cancer in 1983 just as Bill was becoming successful again. Theirs had not been a fairytale marriage – Bill, who never could resist a pretty woman, admits to a number of affairs – but they had always stayed together and made it work. In spite of his lapses, Bill truly loved his wife.

Six years later, in September 1989, he married Tonia Campbell, widow of speed ace Donald Campbell. The couple had first met thirty years earlier when she sang on his TV chat-show *Mostly Maynard*. Although Bill was aleady married to Muriel, he and Tonia had a brief romance. 'A little fling', says Bill. 'Then we disappeared from each other's lives.'

They were reunited all that time later by American comedian Paul Desmond who told Tonia he had met Bill in Australia. Tonia confessed that she still kept a picture of her and Bill together at a première, and Paul told Bill, who looked her up at her Los Angeles home while on a trip to America.

'He came round and drank all my champagne and left at three in the morning', Tonia remembers. And says Bill: 'Thirty years just disappeared. It was sensational.'

None the less he flew back to England without making any commitment. Home again he found a message from Tonia on his answering machine. It said: 'You've run away from me again, and I won't let that happen.' Bill invited her to join him in Leicestershire and asked her to marry him on the night she arrived.

Typically for eccentric Bill, the wedding was not a conventional one and neither is the marriage. The couple spent their wedding night at a boxing tourna-

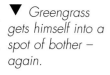

▼ *Greengrass gets himself into a spot of bother – again.*

◄ Now where did he get all that green stuff this time?

▲ Greengrass pride and joy – his big pink American gas-guzzler.

ment in Hull, and throughout their married life Tonia has continued to live in Los Angeles and Bill in Leicestershire. 'We see each other every three or four months', Bill explains. 'She comes over here now – I am too busy to go to LA. It suits us. It's like a honeymoon every time we are together.'

Bill regards his *Heartbeat* role as a great bonus in his later years. 'By the time it came along I'd made all my plans so that I could live on my pensions', says Bill. 'I mean, basically I don't have to work because I have taken out so many pensions when I was earning the big money. So having this has been a bit like winning the pools. It's lovely. It's wonderful when you know you don't have to work, it really is.

'I play Greengrass because it is fun. And if it stops being fun, I can simply not do it any more. But actually this is one of the nicest jobs with the nicest people that I have ever had. And it is probably the most fun ever because there is no responsibility. I can take it or leave it, and it is not all on my back like most of the stuff I have done.'

An essential ingredient in the Greengrass package is his dog Alfred. And Bill, with his band singing background, has made a recording of the Rolling Stones song *Walking the Dog*. The B-side is his version of *Heartbeat*. 'It's very different from Nick's version', he says. 'My record is country and western.' The record, backed by Yorkshire TV, is just another aspect of Greengrass productions. Bill Maynard is an old pro who lives by the time-honoured music hall tradition that you can never milk a good thing too much – on stage or off.

TRAMP
(Alfred)

Tramp, a lurcher with a dodgy history, has been portraying Greengrass's dog Alfred since the beginning of *Heartbeat*.

Tramp is an audience puller, and Yorkshire TV are well aware of his value in the show. He arrives on set chauffeur driven by his personal trainer and brings with him his own travelling bag containing his black custom-made, thermal-lined waterproof coat and a supply of his special food for the duration of his stay – a sudden change in diet upsets his tummy.

The dog has a terrific following among *Heartbeat* viewers, receives fan mail, and is treated with all the reverence due to his celebrity status. When he has to stay overnight on location he is booked into his own hotel room with en-suite bathroom. Even stars Nick Berry and Niamh Cusack make a huge fuss of him.

Not surprisingly Tramp loves every minute of it. According to his owner, he is now quite aware that he is a star. 'It takes him two or three days to come back down to earth when he arrives home off set', says teacher Brenda Tenten. 'He tries to dictate to the rest of the household and has to be retaught that he does not come number one. He thinks he is a star all right.'

To an old showbusiness journalist this kind of display of big star temperament sounds startlingly familiar. So does Tramp have a nice rags to riches story with which to complete the cliché? Of course he does.

'Tramp was found in a very poor state wandering the streets of Manchester',

▶ *Greengrass with Tramp, the dog who reckons he's the real star of the show.*

reveals Brenda. 'He followed a local woman home and would not leave her doorstep. She took him to police kennels and after seven days learned that he had not been claimed and would therefore be put down.

'She didn't want that to happen so she took him home with her. But she lived in a small flat with a cat and she couldn't really keep him permanently. Tramp was a thoroughly unpleasant dog. Apart from anything else, to Tramp, like most lurchers, cats should preferably be between two pieces of bread as a sandwich.

'I have dogs which I take to agility shows – the canine version of show jumping – and this woman took Tramp to a show in Cheshire to try to find him a new owner. Because I already had a lurcher, everyone seemed to assume I would take him on and in the end I did, and I soon lived to regret it.

'It was a real trial at first. He was probably only about eighteen months-old but he looked a bad ten. Tramp had no hair – he still has a very poor coat – he was riddled with worms, he was aggressive to other male dogs and he was sex mad. He tried to mate with everything, including my old and sick cat – which I suppose was preferable to trying to eat her.

'I spent a fortune having him wormed and injected and my other dog spayed and when that still didn't stop his sex attacks I had to have him castrated. I sometimes think the only reason I kept him was because I had spent so much money on him. And he gave absolutely nothing back. It was like having a lodger in the house. He didn't respond to anything. I have had rescue dogs before and I know it can take them quite a long time to start behaving like normal dogs – in Tramp's case it took the best part of two years. I find the fact that he has become a TV star now quite hilarious. I just can't take it seriously at all.'

Lurchers are 'types', not breeds of dogs. A true lurcher is a cross between a sight hound – any hound which hunts by sight rather than smell – and a border collie.

Tramp is aptly named by his owner because of his past and his disreputable appearance, and Brenda believes that he is a classic poachers' or gypsies' lurcher. 'These are traditionally Bedlington terriers crossed with whippets', she says. 'Bedlington terriers are the little woolly dogs which look like lambs and have tassels on their ears – you can see those clearly on Tramp.

'We are pretty sure he had been used for poaching before he was abandoned, perhaps because his coat is so soft and poor they were afraid he wouldn't be tough enough. If you shine a torch he will charge right up the beam which suggests he has been at least partly trained for lamping – which is when animals are trapped in the beam of a light and the dog pounces on them.'

It was in 1987 that Brenda Tenten somewhat reluctantly took the undesirable Tramp into her Huddersfield home. Tramp's showbusiness career began four years later when animal trainer Sue Beale of the Woofers agency was asked by Yorkshire TV if she could find a lurcher for Greengrass in *Heartbeat*.

'I had seen Tramp at dog training classes', she recalls. 'And as soon as I realized the kind of character Greengrass was, I knew that Tramp would be the perfect dog. He is so marvellously scruffy.'

Tramp's acting career was a huge success from the beginning. After seeing rushes of his first ever screen appearance, Keith Richardson was ecstatic. 'That dog is wonderful – I want him in every possible scene', he told his team.

Indeed Tramp's performances as downtrodden Alfred have been totally convincing. On one occasion when Greengrass and Alfred landed in court accused of sheep rustling, Alfred's ability to attract sympathy disrupted filming. The judge told the court that under the Dog Act of 1871 Alfred would be destroyed. 'Awh', said a courtroom extra loudly. Recalls associate producer Pat Brown: 'We had to shoot the whole scene again. But nobody minded. It was just so funny.'

And says Brenda Tenten: 'Every time I see Bill Maynard he says to me: "Just you look after that dog. As long as that dog's all right I know I've still got a job . . ." '

TRICIA PENROSE
(Gina Ward)

To *Heartbeat*'s youngest regular the Sixties are just history. But since being hired to play barmaid Gina, Tricia Penrose has become something of a Sixties fan. She now has a big collection of music from the period, and, to her surprise, has even come to like the fashions. Admits 24-year-old Tricia: 'I think I've been brainwashed. At first I couldn't stand the clothes I had to wear in the series and

▲ The look to melt all the regulars' hearts in the Aidensfield Arms: Tricia Penrose as Gina Ward.

▶ Playing Gina not only converted Tricia to Sixties music but also gave her the opportunity to put her singing talent to use in Heartbeat.

47

now I am beginning to quite like them.

'There seems to be a bit of a revival. You see Sixties-style clothes and shoes in the shops now. I draw the line at hotpants, but I have bought myself a selection of miniskirts as well as a pair of burgundy platform-soled boots that are just like the ones I wear in *Heartbeat*.'

Before being chosen as Gina after an audition at Yorkshire TV's Leeds studio, Liverpudlian Tricia had been seen in smaller roles in several TV series, mostly made in the north of England or the Midlands.

A couple of years ago she played a policewoman in *Brookside* and had an affair with Rod, a policeman who lives in the Close. And it was on *Brookside* that she made her TV début. 'It was the first job I got, when I was just fourteen', she says. 'I played Damon Grant's girlfriend, Ruth.'

Tricia, pert faced, chirpy, and bubbling over with Scouse humour, then went on to win roles in *Emmerdale*, *Medics* and *Boon*. She once played a small part in *Coronation Street*, as the receptionist at the hotel that Ken and Alma visited for an ill-fated break over New Year 1993. 'That was my dream come true – I always wanted to be in the *Street*', she says. 'More recently I was asked to go for an audition for a bigger role but I couldn't at the time because I was working on *Heartbeat*. Just fate, I suppose. Naturally I couldn't quit *Heartbeat* – but it would have been lovely if the timing had been different and I could have done both . . . '

Tricia at one time supplemented her acting work by being part of an unusual double act. She used to sing in pubs and clubs around her home town of Kirkby in partnership with her mother.

'Mum and I were called Second Image, but I went on to sing with other bands and I was part of a duo called Impulse – like the deodorant. Now I have been working on doing some recordings with the company which records Take That and hope to have something released soon.'

Quick to make use of all the talent going, the producers of Yorkshire have twice called upon Tricia to sing in the show. They even put Gina into a talent contest – which she won, of course.

Tricia has a steady boyfriend, Irish Liverpudlian Jason Gallagher, who with his father runs a local nightclub. She still lives in Liverpool with her gran. 'I help look after her', she says.

Since discovering the joys of Sixties music Tricia plays her collection all the time. 'I have been very lucky', she explains. 'A *Heartbeat* fan in Goathland recorded his whole enormous collection for me. And the more I listen the more it grows on me . . . ' And so Tricia, like so many of the young viewers of *Heartbeat*, is discovering through the programme the joys of an age which was over before she was born.

STUART GOLLAND
(George Ward)

Stuart Golland has no doubts about why he was chosen to play the landlord of The Aidensfield Arms. 'I twisted the producer's arm', he says.

For 49-year-old Stuart the role of George Ward is his biggest acting break. 'I was being interviewed at Yorkshire with the possibility that I might make some guest appearances in episodes of this new series when the producer mentioned the fairly small but regular part of the pub landlord', recalls Stuart. 'I quite fancied some regular work, and I had run a pub myself, so I reckoned I knew what it was all about. I kept plugging away and eventually they gave me the part. Since then the whole thing has grown and grown.'

Yorkshireman Stuart began his working life in the building trade and was a plasterer for twelve years. While employed on a plastering contract on the Isle of Man in 1968 he took a job as a part-time pub barman in the evenings. 'It was to pass the time – I didn't really need extra money, but I was bored', he says. 'Then they made me manager of the pub.'

Stuart finally quit the building trade to become bar manager of the Top Rank Club in Sheffield in 1970. It was opposite the Crucible Theatre, and marked the beginning of his love affair with acting: 'All the actors used to come across to our club, so I began to get interested.'

But acting seemed unattainable as a career and George decided he wanted to totally change his life and travelled to Cardiff to join the Merchant Navy. 'It

◄ *Stuart Golland as George Ward, in pensive mood.*

49

▲ *Dressed to drink: George in his Sunday best.*

sounds crazy, but the ship never came in', he says. 'I ended up enrolling in a drama course at the Welsh College of Music and Drama. It really was from one extreme to another.'

He found work as a scene shifter in theatre in Cardiff and became firmly bitten by the showbusiness bug. 'I happened to see Peter Brook's famous production of *A Midsummer Night's Dream*, with Ben Kingsley and Frances de la Tour, and that was it', he recalls. 'I was hooked.'

In 1973 he applied for a job in fringe theatre after spotting an advertisement in the magazine *Time Out*. He was hired. And he says: 'I have been pretty fortunate, in the twenty years or so since then I have rarely been out of work, and I even had a year at the National Theatre working with people like Eric Porter for whom I understudied in *Cat on a Hot Tin Roof*. But I never earned much money and certainly *Heartbeat* has been my biggest break.'

Stuart, who lives in Leeds with his social worker wife Frances, has had small roles in a number of TV series including *Waterfront Beat* (the police series set in Liverpool in which he played a sergeant) *Stay Lucky*, *Emmerdale*, *Rumpole* and *Coronation Steet*. In the *Street* he played the tycoon who bought Ken Barlow's newspaper when he had to sell to settle with Deirdre.

During the Sixties Stuart was working as a plasterer in Newquay in Cornwall, but he does not look back on that era with any great nostalgia – for him the Nineties are proving to be the best time of his life. 'I am doing what I want to do.'

PETER FIRTH
(Dr James Radcliffe)

The role of Dr Radcliffe from Whitby, introduced in the fourth series of *Heartbeat*, marks a new venture for actor Peter Firth. He is forty years old and has an impressive film and theatre pedigree – but this is his first regular adult part in a major long-running TV drama. His only other lengthy TV run was as a young lad in *The Flaxton Boys*.

Says producer Martyn Auty, who was responsible for bringing Peter into the show: 'He is a fine actor and we feel we are very lucky to have him in the series. Peter Firth is a prestigious actor.'

Peter, more recently appearing in outstanding British films like *Letter to Brezhnev* and Richard Attenborough's *Shadowlands*, first gained recognition in 1973 when he catapulted spectacularly on to the London stage at the National Theatre playing Alan Strang in *Equus*. He was just twenty years old and his performance was a triumph. As well as critical acclaim he gained vast press coverage because of the long and controversial nude scene he played in *Equus*. When his Yorkshire parents came to see the play in London he says: 'They

▶ *The new doctor from Whitby: Peter Firth as James Radcliffe.*

51

pretended to be very broad-minded about it but I knew better.'

He went with the play to Broadway and was nominated for a Tony award. There followed several more successes at the National before he switched mainly to film.

Peter was born and bred in Yorkshire – his parents ran a pub near Pudsey. For more than twenty years he has lived in London, but he is now renting a cottage on the Yorkshire Moors, in the middle of *Heartbeat* country.

'Strangely enough it was pure coincidence and nothing to do with *Heartbeat* that prompted us to move up to Yorkshire', says Peter. 'We had already been in the cottage for some months when the *Heartbeat* job was offered to me. It was as if my career had in some way followed me. It was very odd.'

And, also by coincidence, his parents now live in Whitby, the home and work-place of his *Heartbeat* character.

Peter reckons he is still getting the hang of his character, and settling in among a crew and cast who have been together a long time. He had always deliber-ately steered clear of long-running TV series and, indeed, has made sure he has been able to carry on with other work. He was given a six-week break during the filming of the fourth *Heartbeat* series so that he could accept a role in a film made in Dublin of Beryl Bainbridge's novel *An Awfully Big Adventure*, co-starring Alan Rickman.

'I was delighted to be offered *Heartbeat* because ultimately I decided I have been doing this job long enough and done enough different work to get away with it now', he says. 'I wanted to do something that everybody liked. And *Heartbeat* certainly seems to fit that bill. Previously I had always been afraid of being labelled.'

He has not decided yet whether he wants to settle permanently in Yorkshire. 'We have kept our place in London and are working out what we should do', he says. 'We like it up north but the problem is that it is so far away from every-where else – and the climate puts us off a bit.'

Peter has been married for four years to his second wife, actress Lindsey Readman, and they have two young children. He also has a thirteen-year-old son – whom he describes as 'thirteen going on forty' – from his first marriage.

Peter went to Hanson High School where he first became interested in theatre, taking weekly Saturday morning acting lessons at Bradford Civic Theatre Drama Club and doing the odd walk-on part for Yorkshire TV.

When he was fifteen his headmaster gave permission for him to play one of the leads in *The Flaxton Boys*, a BBC children's television serial.

'The idea was that I should return to school, but no way was I going back', he recalls. 'I wasn't very bright and not very interested, and I was a bit naughty. I was only any good at gymnastics. I didn't see the point in going back.'

He acquired a London agent and started a career which was to take him thou-sands of miles from his native Yorkshire, appearing in films all over the world. Only now does he appear to be coming full circle. 'And it's strange how many people do, isn't it?', he says.

FRANK MIDDLEMASS
(Dr Alex Ferrenby)

Frank Middlemass was seventy-three years-old when his *Heartbeat* character Dr Ferrenby was killed off in a fishing accident. But veteran actor Frank has no intention of quietly fading away. 'Actors never retire, my dear', he booms. 'I've been very busy lately – and that's the way I like it.'

His voice is from a bygone age: uncorrupted English public school. 'My family was very prosperous when I was a boy', he explains. 'Not any more – but they were then. My father was a director of a Liverpool shipping company, as was his father before him.

'The war took me away from home. I had five years in the army during the war and then another four in Egypt afterwards. My demob kept getting deferred.

'But it was all for the best really because I had known from when I was a small boy that all I wanted to do was to act – and in my family that wouldn't do at all. I had to wait for people to die – notably my mama. She would never have let me go on the stage. Never! She considered acting to be the equivalent of going on the streets and I really did have to wait for her to die before I could do it.

'You didn't argue with my mama – and that was how things stayed, however old you became. Age had nothing to do with it. She expected you to abide by her will, and you did.

'After she died that made me a free man and I argued my way into a rep company in Penzance, right at the bottom end of Cornwall, and learned my trade that way. I had two wonderful years and I knew I had been right – it was the only career for me.

'I still love acting. The more I am working the happier I am.'

Frank is one of the best-known faces on TV, and he became a household voice in the Eighties when he took over the BBC radio role of Dan Archer. He played Dan from 1982 until the famous Ambridge farmer collapsed while tending a sheep and died of a heart attack in 1986, supposedly aged eighty-nine.

'That's the only thing about my career – I always seem to die', says Frank.

He is a regular in *As Time Goes By*, the popular sit-com starring Judi Dench and Geoffrey Palmer, in which he plays Geoffrey's father. He still enjoys theatre and spent the early part of 1994 working at London's King's Head Theatre.

'I actually think it is work which holds you together', he says. 'It's when people retire that things start falling apart and people have heart attacks. That's probably what happened to poor old Ferrenby. It was after handing the practice over to Kate that he died.'

Frank lives alone in Chiswick, West London. He was born and brought up on Teesside and says he fell in love with the north of England all over again while working on *Heartbeat*.

'I felt I had a wonderful part in a wonderful show', he says. 'I would have carried on for as long as they wanted me. But once Ferrenby had handed the prac-

53

tice over to Kate that put the writing on the wall.' He regrets the passing of Ferrenby but says he understands it. 'Shows like *Heartbeat* have to move on, and Ferrenby was an old man. Like me.'

Nonetheless Frank intends to keep his work schedule as demanding as ever.

◀ *Frank Middlemass as Dr Alex Ferrenby, everybody's idea of a country GP.*

▶ *Dr Ferrenby's passion for fishing was eventually to cause his tragic death.*

5

AT THE STATION

—

DEREK FOWLDS
(Sergeant Oscar Blaketon)

On the set of *Heartbeat* they are known as 'The Lads' – the three actors who play the policemen at Ashfordly police station around whom PC Rowan's working life revolves.

Leader of the pack is Derek Fowlds – a man with a chequered past. In the late Sixties and early Seventies he became famous as Mr Derek – partner of the TV puppet Basil Brush. Then he went on to even greater fame as Bernard, principal private secretary to Paul Eddington, in the hit sit-coms *Yes Minister*, and *Yes Prime Minister*.

Now as Sergeant Blaketon in *Heartbeat*, 57-year-old Derek reckons he has found the role of a lifetime. And, as he always does with characters that he plays, he has invented a whole life story for the crotchety policeman with a heart of gold, taking Blaketon's background a lot further than Yorkshire TV ever attempted.

'I do it to give the characters a kind of shape and reality for me', he says. 'I use what we know about them from the scripts and then embellish it in my mind. After all, if they are to exist they must be born, have a family, go to school.

'Blaketon was born in Haworth in Yorkshire and went into the army before joining the police force. I reckon his father died during the 1914–18 war when he

55

was still a small child and then four years later his mother died and he was taken to live in Leeds. He joined up while he was still very young and the army became his family.

'When he was demobbed he went straight into the police force and was posted to Ashfordly. He fell in love with and married a village girl who left him for a younger man, the local butcher, and they had one son. We saw Blaketon's son in the third series of *Heartbeat* and so another side to him was actually introduced on screen with that.

'And I have a theory about his long-running feud with Greengrass – Greengrass's sister was his wife's mother, you see. And they were at loggerheads from the beginning, it was a family thing.

'Blaketon loves to listen to Glenn Miller – that's his solace. He had loved his wife dearly, and when she left him he became a social recluse and the complete professional twenty-four-hours-a-day policeman. He adores his son and does not see him as often as he would like, and secretly he would love to marry again but doesn't know how to go about it.

'At the moment he is worried because his policing career is coming to an end. He has only got about four years to go before he retires, and he doesn't know what to do then.

'Actually I believe Blaketon will retire and get a caravan on Whitby beach and set himself up as a private detective. And I reckon Yorkshire ought to make a TV series about him then and call it *The Blaketon Files*.

'I love the man. I like him a lot. I want to explore every facet of him. Every layer of him.'

Derek also invented a life-story for *Yes Minister*'s Bernard. 'Bernard was a thoroughly upper-class chap who went to Marlborough and Trinity College, Oxford, and was a classics scholar', he says. 'I was interviewed once by Australian TV who wanted to know about the difference between me and Bernard. They asked if I was anything like him. I had to say that we were completely different and that the main difference was that at the time he was supposed to be thirty-six and I was actually fifty-two. I must have been the oldest Parliamentary Private Secretary in history.'

Derek's early life could not have been further removed from Bernard's. 'I was a secondary modern school boy', he says. 'I came from a working-class background and went to school in Berkhamsted. I certainly never went to university. I left school at fifteen and became an apprentice printer. Then I worked in a factory and did my national service in the RAF, as a wireless operator. That was when I started performing – a lot of people started in the services in those days. Afterwards I won a scholarship to RADA and I was there at the same time as Sarah Miles and Edward Fox.

'The Sixties were my golden years. It was the beginning of my career and a very wonderful ten years. I was young and intense, very ambitious and single-minded – almost blinkered.

'I did four years in rep while the rest of the world went on outside and I hardly

▲ 'The Lads': William
Simons, Derek Fowlds
and Mark Jordon on
the set of Heartbeat.

▲ 'Evenin' all.'
But Derek Fowlds'
Sergeant Blaketon
is a bit gruffer
than old George
Dixon.

noticed it. Then I went to Broadway in *Chips with Everything* and I will never forget that opening night. People were standing on their seats and cheering – we got about fifteen curtain calls, or at least that's what it felt like. It was amazing.'

Derek has been married twice. His first wife was diplomat's daughter Wendy Tory, and he has two sons from that marriage: James, 30, father of Derek's four-year-old grandson Jacob, and Jeremy, 26, also an actor. In 1974 he married *Blue Peter* presenter Lesley Judd and was devastated when the marriage ended after less than a year. After this experience he vowed never to marry again. 'To be divorced once is an error; to be divorced twice is rather inexcusable', he says.

He now lives with his long-time girlfriend, a schoolteacher called Jo. They divide their time between homes in London's Battersea and near Bath and he says they both agree that marriage would spoil a beautiful relationship. 'We have been together for eighteen years and we are happy the way we are, so why risk it all?' he asks. 'Anyway, whenever I think I want to get married she doesn't, and whenever she wants to I don't . . . '

When Derek decided in 1973 to part company with Basil Brush, the fox loved by millions of children, there followed a long lean period. It was his toughest time in a career which until then had been a busy one.

'Basil was huge', he says. 'We did eight series and two Royal Command Performances, and to this day people say hello Mr Derek – even after *Yes*

▲ *Blaketon and Greengrass have a long-standing dislike for each other. And Derek Fowlds reckons he knows the reason why . . .*

Minister and now *Heartbeat* and all else that I have done. After I gave up Basil my only hope was to go back into the theatre because I was so well known as Basil's partner that it was hard to get work.

'In those days it was very easy to get typecast. You don't seem to hear that word any more. People like David Jason jump from one big series to another. It didn't used to be like that. You got stuck. And if you were a big telly name they wouldn't let you do commercials either, so you missed out on the big cash they get now.

'It was 1979 before I did the pilot for *Yes Minister*, and that was a long hard gap. I had to find other work to earn a living and I drove a mini-cab for a while. But I was always an actor driving a mini-cab. I never gave up. And my first job after that bad spell was playing Hamlet.'

Derek is delighted now to be doing straight roles on TV. There is humour in Blaketon, but *Heartbeat* remains a serious drama programme.

He made a deliberate decision to try to change the course of his career after finishing with *Yes Prime Minister* in 1988: 'I did a play in Australia that year and came back and decided I wanted to get back into film and TV drama. I got an agent who told me it could take five years because I was so established in comedy. On stage, in particular, I was best known for farces.

'Slowly but surely I began to guest in TV dramas like *Van der Valk*, *Perfect Scoundrels*, and *Darling Buds of May*. I began to get back to my first love — drama. Blaketon has been the icing on the cake.

▲ Yes, Blaketon can smile – just.

◀Blaketon often gives Nick a hard time, but he has a sneaking liking for the young PC.

'I always talk about the Quentin Crisp factor in acting. When John Hurt played Quentin Crisp it was a performance which put him on a different level. That can happen at any age which is one of the good things about our business.

'I don't believe that has happened to me yet. I am still waiting for my Quentin Crisp. Meanwhile Blaketon has been very good to me. I owe him a great deal.'

And yet Derek was astonished to be offered the role in the first place. 'It came about because I was having dinner with Caroline Dawson, my agent, and Malcolm Drury the casting director who was just casting the first *Heartbeat*, although I didn't know that or anything about it at the time.

'We were just chatting when suddenly in the middle of dinner he said: "I've just had an idea." But he wouldn't elaborate on it. Then about a week later Caroline told me she thought Yorkshire were going to offer me a part in a series. Now I'd never been a regular – I don't count *Yes Prime Minister* or *Yes Minister* because they only took up eight weeks of the year. I had never been a regular in a series that occupies you for half the year or more.

'This was a whole new thing and I duly went to Yorkshire and read the script and I thought: "Well, this is great, but why me? I'm a Londoner from Clapham Common and there are so many wonderful northern actors."

'I remember asking them if they realized I wasn't a northerner and they said "You're a bloody actor, aren't you?" They hired me anyway – and I was thrilled.

'But I never imagined we would make this many episodes and that we would be pulling in sixteen or seventeen million viewers.'

MARK JORDON
(PC Phil Bellamy)

PC Bellamy is the youngest of the team at Ashfordly police station, and can be a bit of a handful. He is supposed to be about twenty-four and in many ways acts younger than his years. Bellamy couldn't be more different from 29-year-old Mark Jordon, the Lancashire actor who plays him. Mark may boast boyish good looks – but he had to grow up young. He didn't get a choice.

His mother was an unmarried teenager who later developed chronic arthritis. She is now confined to a wheelchair and became progressively more disabled as Mark was growing up. 'I was brought up by just my mum and my nan – my grandmother – so I know everything about running a house', he says. 'I know how to wash, how to iron, how to cook.'

It was not an easy childhood. Mark had to play his part in every aspect of running the home. 'My mum spent a lot of time in hospital and then my nan used to come to stay', he says. 'I was brought up by both of them about equally.'

Ironically there was a connection with the police which Mark remembers playing a big part in his childhood. When she was well enough, his mother worked for many years as a civilian secretary at Oldham police station and Mark was given an early insight into what police work was really all about.

'Mum used to take me along to the police station when I was at school and they all tucked me under their wing and gave me a good time, looking after me and showing me this office and that office.

▲ *Mark Jordon as Bellamy, the boy bobby.*

'I remember realizing how boring it was most of the time, and that's why there really is inclined to be a lot of fun going on in a police station. You have to have a sense of humour doing that job, otherwise you are going to hate it. Certainly in the days when I was going to Oldham police station it seemed there was a lot of high jinks going on to pass the time because there is always a lot of waiting about just in case. And in *Heartbeat* my character is often in charge of the micky taking, and that makes it a good part to play.

'By the time I was about fifteen or sixteen they used to invite me down to the local shooting range and I got to let off a few live rounds and things like that. It was a luxury for a little lad in Oldham.

'I don't think I'd better name the policemen, though. I should think they were breaking all the rules. I doubt they'd do it nowadays the way crime is going on at the moment. When you think about it you could just turn a gun on them.

'I spent a hell of a lot of time with them, and I think my mother was hoping I might become a policeman – a bit of security and all of that. But I had already made up my mind that I wanted to be an actor. I was quite sure of that.'

Mark's first job when he left school was working in a painter and decorator's shop. He got involved in youth theatre, and then won a place at the famous Oldham Theatre Workshop which has produced so many top young northern actors including, over the years, almost all of the younger members of the cast of *Coronation Street*.

True to the Workshop's form, Mark has appeared in the *Street* – as a police-

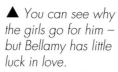

▲ *You can see why the girls go for him – but Bellamy has little luck in love.*
▶ *Bellamy and Nick on the case.*

man. 'I played PC Best', he says. 'I was there for the burglary at Mavis and Derek's, for the break-in at the Barlows', and when Tracy went missing. I obviously look right in uniform.'

To get his Equity card in the first place Mark set up a theatre group with some friends and performed in Lancashire pubs and clubs. 'It was a bit of a struggle to begin with', he recalls. 'But having been brought up in a house full of ladies stood me in good stead in my early acting days when I was skint and waiting for jobs because at least I knew how to cater for myself and look after myself.'

But there was also a disadvantage to his all-female upbringing: 'My girlfriend has to tell me about football', he says. 'I haven't the foggiest what is going on. There was nobody to take me to the terraces on a Saturday afternoon and I didn't even learn to play it properly.

'Actually we have a role-reversal thing, my girlfriend and me. I have to tell her which cycle to put the washer on and I do all the cooking while she sits and watches the telly on a Sunday. Then I start tut-tutting because she's watching the football again.'

Mark still lives in Oldham, not far from his mum, with girlfriend Debbie Jackson, who has recently left college with a media degree.

His first real acting break came when producer Marilyn Fox cast him in a BBC children's series called *Seaview*. In between the last two series of *Heartbeat*, Mark did another BBC children's series and worked again with the woman who gave him that first break.

He is happy to stick with *Heartbeat* for as long as the show runs, and, in fact, says he cannot believe his good fortune. 'I have been a very lucky boy', he says. 'Not only am I involved in something that is successful, but I am having a damn good time while I am doing it.

'Also, *Heartbeat* seems to be going on and on. It was four years ago now that I was auditioned. I met the then director and producer and the casting director, got a recall, and, surprise, surprise, got the job.

'By acting standards this one seems like a never-ending job, which is like heaven, because in this profession you don't often come across that. And there is an added attraction because you get long-enough breaks in between each series to do something else. I have done a bit of theatre between each *Heartbeat*.'

Mark feels he has been particularly fortunate because he faced a brief hiatus in his career when he stopped looking like a boy. His fresh-faced, boyish looks won him jobs playing lads far younger than he was well into his twenties.

'I always played the roguish Jack-the-lad and seemed to play young teenagers for ever. I think it was the freckles. Then suddenly it didn't work any more: I started to look like a man. I wasn't sure how that would affect me.

'So Bellamy has been a great opportunity for me. I am still playing someone a few years younger than me but at least he is a grown man – well, more or less: he's a cheeky chappy.'

WILLIAM SIMONS
(PC Alf Ventress)

The third member of the Ashfordly police team is Constable Alf Ventress, a real old-fashioned copper, played by William Simons.

'He is a lazy chap who has been a police constable all his life and will end up as that and nothing more', says William. 'He enjoys a smoke and he loves his food and he likes a nice quiet life and that's about it.'

Will, 52, who lives in Fulham, south-west London, with his wife Janie, has made something of a career of playing policemen – particularly recently. Through much of the winter of 1993–94 he appeared on both channels on Sunday nights in top police shows. As well as playing PC Ventress in *Heartbeat* he also played Inspector Alleyn's right-hand man, Inspector Fox, in the BBC series. 'At least it meant I couldn't lose in the ratings war', he says.

In the 1980s William starred as Detective Constable Thackeray in *Cribb*, the Victorian detective series. Thackeray was another plodding cop and portraying him landed William in trouble with his wife. 'I had to grow a beard and she

63

hated it', he recalls. 'She is very anti facial hair.'

In spite of playing three important TV cops Will claims he has never compared them with each other. 'I don't even watch myself on TV', he says. 'I am too critical.'

William was born and educated in South Wales, the son of a solicitor, and says he has always been unable to escape the clutches of the law: 'I was a counsel in *Crown Court* – if I am not representing the law in one way on television I seem to be doing it in another.'

Now a dedicated Londoner, he has thoroughly enjoyed working in Yorkshire and fallen in love with Goathland. 'Only the cold puts me off a bit', he says. 'I'm afraid I am a soft southerner.'

◄*Director Tim Dowd goes through a scene with Nick Berry and William Simons during shooting of Series 4.*

▶ *William Simons as Ventress in typical hyperactive pose.*

6

THE SIXTIES LOOK OF *HEARTBEAT*

—

The Sixties look of *Heartbeat* is a major part of its appeal. Yet, say the men and women who put it together, quite a lot of it is a cheat. This may come as a shock, but the truth, apparently, is that if the series were totally authentic it just would not look right on the small screen.

The clothes, the wallpaper, and the hairstyles and make-up are all tailored to modern television. Their flavour is of the Sixties, but that is about the limit of it.

Even Nick Berry's police uniform is a cheat. 'He should really be wearing a cape because capes and not mackintoshes were regulation issue in North Yorkshire up until 1966, and when *Heartbeat* began it was fairly clearly placed in 1965 and we haven't let it move on really', says Martin Baugh. 'As a result we frequently get letters from retired policemen pointing this out.

'But we don't think Nick would look right in a cape. It would be too period – people associate policemen in capes with Sherlock Holmes. It would be quite off-putting to the modern eye, particularly to all the kids who watch *Heartbeat*. And Nick would find a cape very disturbing. So we pretend that Nick's part of North Yorkshire was issued with the new uniform a year or two early as a trial run. And yes – we actually do write to people to explain this.'

Heartbeat's fashion clothes are also subtly amended to suit the programme makers' purposes. 'If you used the real colours of the time it would be a disaster', says Martin. 'Carnaby Street colours of the late Sixties look terribly garish to

◀Gina is
definitely a Sixties
chick: is that a
skirt or a belt?

▶ Even Kate has
at least one
miniature mini in
her wardrobe.

the modern eye. What we do is create an illusion – which really is a posh way of saying we cheat.

'We go for the flavour of the time – not the fact. As far as the clothes go we have two groups of people. These are country people and anyone over about thirty-five is going to be wearing the sort of clothes that country people wear which don't have a lot to do with any particular period. More pastel colours for a start.

'We can have a bit of fun with the younger ones, particularly Gina.'

Gina appears in the series in the miniskirts and hotpants of the time – but even such apparently obvious Sixties styles as these are full of hidden dangers.

'*Heartbeat* is a bit vague on its exact time scale and we have to be careful because tights only came in 1965 and that was the start of the miniskirt because miniskirts couldn't happen until tights were in all the shops. Before 1965 you could only get dancers' tights from specialist shops.

'We have actually put Gina in hotpants more than in miniskirts because they are safer and easier for the cameraman', says Martin. 'If she has to bend down or something it's OK with hotpants, but in a miniskirt you have problems.'

Very few of the clothes seen in *Heartbeat* are authentic Sixties items. 'We find

▲ *Moorland cop: Nick Berry wearing a post-1966 police uniform, adapted for the sake of modern television audiences.*

Sixties garments and then we almost always get them copied because most of them were so badly made they would just fall apart with the kind of use we give them', explains Martin. 'The fabrics have faded. There was a lot of plastic around in 1967–68 and that is now all sticking together and quite impossible to use. A lot of Sixties clothes were rubbish – made to be thrown away. And don't forget, we are talking about clothes that are around thirty years-old.'

Nonetheless, Martin's search for authenticity is an extensive one. His quest takes him regularly to Paris, which he has found to be a rich source of suitable clothing. 'There is a company there which has a lot of Sixties gear and it is interesting to see how little difference there is between the French stuff and the English. After all these episodes we have been through the entire stock in this country, and I discovered that in France there is about a third as much as the agents have got here.

'One person who does wear Sixties originals occasionally is Gina – when we can get stuff in reasonably good condition. Some things you can just buy off the peg today. Kids in Yorkshire then would mostly have only had access to what was available in local shops, and there weren't any trendy shops in North Yorkshire. It was the way they put clothes together that made the look of the time for them – just like layering now, wearing your waistcoat outside your jacket or whatever.

'A very common look at the time was a V-neck sweater over a polo-neck sweater – but these were perfectly ordinary garments you could get anywhere. Knitwear from the Sixties is nearly always perished and we need a lot of that because it is so cold in Yorkshire where we film.'

The Yorkshire climate has governed many of the *Heartbeat* fashions – particulary for Niamh Cusack. Although her fur-lined duffel coat was introduced because of the discomfort she experienced, Martin Baugh deliberated long and hard about allowing Niamh's character, Dr Kate, to wear trousers quite as much as she does. 'There is no doubt she wears them more than a doctor in North Yorkshire in those days really would have done', he says, 'but they are there to keep Niamh warm. Trousers for women were fine by then and she would have worn them socially – but maybe not for work. She might have put on a pair of trousers and her wellies if she was called out to a farm somewhere, but I suspect that would have been all. And she certainly would not have worn them in the surgery. We do, in fact, try to keep Niamh out of trousers in the surgery – but if there is a sequence where she goes off on the moors straight after a surgery scene then I am afraid we have to bend the rules.'

The Sixties was a period of distinctive hairstyles, and in this too the *Heartbeat* interpretation has been strongly influenced by practicalities as well as by history.

Says make-up and hair designer Judy Jarvis: 'We changed Niamh's hair after the first series for a number of reasons. As far as the programme went she had matured quite a lot in the second series so we didn't want all that backcombed hair. We wanted it to be more natural and we wanted her to be more at home with her hair – she had never liked the backcombed look and felt strongly that it didn't suit her. We wanted her hair to swing and look shiny in the second series – a sort of classic Sixties look which suits her very well.

'But there was another reason for the change: the original hairstyle proved just too difficult to maintain when we were shooting. The Yorkshire weather, all that wind, played havoc with it. We decided to come up with a hairstyle which would keep going for twelve hours in the snow and rain.

'It makes sense too for a busy doctor. No working woman of any era in history would want a hairdo which took forty-five minutes to put together. And you have to remember that in spite of all the long hair on the streets, the police and hospitals and institutions like that were stricter about length of hair in the Sixties than they are now. Women police officers were not allowed to wear any make-up – and of course they are now. It was the same with nurses: in the Sixties their hair had to be off the collar and they were not allowed to wear make-up and have hair all over the place.

'We can have a bit more fun with the crowd scenes. You can do the back-combing and all the business with the local girls. We cut hair as well, and if we get the chance we do a Beatles haircut like a shot. But with hair as well everything was a lot more behind up here in Yorkshire than it was in swinging London so you have to tone it down a bit.

'We are fortunate that *Heartbeat* is not moving into the Seventies because then there was much longer hair and sideboards and things. As it is we can use extras more or less as they look today – you just backcomb the lady's hair and give them a paler lipstick or something and that is enough to create the illusion.

'Long, curly, layered hair is my biggest problem. In the Sixties you couldn't have curly hair, come what may. Women went to extraordinary lengths to straighten their hair out. So when we get extras with lots of curls it is really not going to be acceptable and we have to work miracles. We usually try to pile curly hair on top of their heads and put it into a backcombed bun or something.

'With the principal characters you have to think it all out very carefully. We are aiming for the mood of the Sixties, not the actuality.

'With make-up it's exactly the same. We go the whole hog when we can, like with Gina, but Niamh really does look horrendous in a very pale lipstick so that is why we darken hers – we want to keep her in the Sixties mood but we want her looking attractive as well.

'Gina can wear the pale orange and have the big black eyes.'

Judy has two women working with her in her department: make-up supervisor Jill Rogerson, who is in charge of continuity, and make-up assistant Alison Philpot. 'Alison always makes Niamh up', says Judy. 'You can't pass make-ups backwards and forwards because although you could describe the look and tell someone exactly what materials you have used, no two people would do it exactly the same.

'Also there is a great personal relationship between make-up and the artists. The first face the actor sees in the morning is his make-up person.'

Sixties sets are relatively easy to come across in Yorkshire, according to set

▲ *Nick and
Kate display
typical Sixties
outfits outside their
police house
home.*

designer Andrew Sanderson. Problems come with what must not be seen rather than what can. 'There are houses in North Yorkshire that we have gone into and not had to change a thing – they are still exactly the way they were in the Sixties. A lot of rural property around here is lived in by tenant farmers or farm workers and the places haven't been touched before', he says.

'Goathland was perfect – it's like going into a time warp. But there are always hidden dangers you have to watch out for. The bane of my life are those big round bales of silage you get everywhere nowadays piled in huge heaps and all covered in shiny black plastic. That stuff shows up on camera three miles away – and it certainly didn't exist in the Sixties. I go around with about ten tarpaulins all the time ready to cover the stuff up.

'You also have to watch out for double yellow lines – technically they did come in around 1965–66, but certainly not in rural Yorkshire. Then there are burglar alarm boxes. We are always having to cover those up.

◀ *(Far Left) Kate with classic Sixties beehive in the first series. (Left) Gina in full make-up.*

▼ *The design team reconstruct Gina's bedroom to make it as authentic-looking as possible – with impressive results.*

71

'I have one assistant designer whose job it is to stay by the camera, keep her eye on every shot and spot anything like that we have missed. Her name is Anne Bega and she is a terrier, a stickler.

'We need that though, because people love to catch us out. And nowadays with everyone having a videorecorder it's much easier. There are people, who if they think there is a mistake in a show will whizz back and freeze frame a shot to check.

'Now we take a lot of trouble with the cars. Not only must they be in period but they all have to be roadworthy, taxed, insured and so on, because we need to use them on public roads. The Rowans' Triumph and all the other vehicles are absolutely right for the period. But we have viewers who are quite fanatical. We once used a Land Rover which was absolutely perfect, but some bloke wrote in to say the sidelamp was wrong – our vehicle had a sidelamp which didn't come in until 1968 or something. I went back and studied the film and in order to see this lamp he must have had the programme on video and stopped the tape and gone backwards and forwards goodness knows how many times.

'Radial tyres are another thing you have to watch out for. They didn't come in until later. You wouldn't think people would notice a thing like tyres, but believe me they do.'

Acquiring the *Heartbeat* vehicles is the job of production buyer David Eaton – in fact he is responsible for finding all manner of materials and creatures called for by the scripts. 'I'm a scavenger – I'll buy, borrow or rent', he says. 'And as I have a limited budget I am always looking for something for nothing.'

Yorkshire TV now actually own four of the cars used in *Heartbeat*: Niamh's green Triumph Herald, Nick's red vintage MG TA, Gina's scarlet bubble-car, and the black Ford Anglia which becomes the station police car in the fourth series.

Says David: 'I decided to buy the bubble-car, the Triumph and the Anglia because we use them so much it would end up cheaper than renting. But in the case of the MG I couldn't find anybody to rent me one.

'This is the car which Nick finds as a wreck in a barn and rebuilds. So in the end I bought a model which was in reasonable roadworthy condition so that we could take it apart and then gradually rebuild it. It's getting to be beautiful now, much better than when we bought it.

'Other vehicles which we use occasionally are rented through a specialist called Mark Harrison who finds and maintains them for us. He has found us a car and repainted it all in eight hours before now. We always seem to be working at speed.

'Nick's motor bike, a Frances Barnet, an old classic British model, is also rented. He keeps it, of course, because it is so much Nick Rowan, even though in the fourth series the station gets its first police car. We have stuck absolutely to the history of the North Yorkshire police force here.

'Until 1966 only station sergeants had cars – like Blaketon's Ford Prefect. They were sometimes made available to other officers, but they were actually issued specifically to the sergeants. In 1966–67 station cars like our Anglia were brought in. They were the step before the blue and white Panda cars, which were not introduced in North Yorkshire until 1969.'

Keeping the authenticity of the medical side of *Heartbeat* is also a responsibility of David Eaton's. 'All the equipment used in Niamh's surgery and in the Whitby Hospital has to be authentic Sixties medical equipment', he explains. 'There are specialist agencies, two in particular that I use, Film and Medical Services and Casts, which rent out medical equipment from all periods.'

David acquires many items from private collectors. He says the most difficult thing he was ever asked to find was a set of toby jugs of World War One leaders required in the first series of *Heartbeat*.

'By chance I found that a set was about to be auctioned by Christies', he recalls. 'I couldn't afford to buy them – they fetched more than £8,000 – but in the end I managed to persuade the owner to lend them to me in return for a fee and a pledge that they would be returned undamaged. I slept with those toby jugs.'

Most of the interior sets used in *Heartbeat* are genuine interior rooms in private houses. Recently the house used as Ashfordly police station changed hands and a duplicate has been built in a warehouse in Leeds. The interior of Dr Kate's Aidensfield surgery has also been built within the same warehouse.

'This is a quite common thing to do nowadays and we are doing the same with the interior of the new doctor's surgery in the fourth series', says Andrew. 'We have copied the police station absolutely. One of the tricks is to make sure you build a proper room with four walls and a ceiling all nailed together. If you don't do that it looks like a set with shots coming from impossible angles. And the sound is wrong too.'

Yorkshire employ two location managers on *Heartbeat*: Mary Rotherham and David Nightingale. Their job is to seek out appropriate locations for each episode. Some locations have stayed the same from the very beginning – like the house in Askwith which is used as the police house, Nick and Kate's home. This house is owned by a nurse called Debbie Walker who over *Heartbeat*'s extended run has learned to live with the demands of film-making.

'I think she now regards us as part of her family', says Mary. 'When she was ill in hospital recently we all visited her. If she is late home somebody feeds her rabbits and guinea-pigs and things.

'She continues living in her cottage throughout filming and we have taken over virtually her whole house. She is left with just one bedroom and even that is full of our junk during the day but she doesn't seem to mind. She is away all day at work anyway. For the fourth series we built a replica of her bathroom in the warehouse in Leeds, so at least she can have that back.

'Often we use different locations for different parts of the same building in the series. Greengrass's cottage in Goathland is actually two cottages. We use one with a fairly untidy outside which is quite smart inside for the exterior shots, and the interior shots are done in another cottage which is the other way round.

'Kitchens are the biggest problems. The first thing anybody has modernized in their home is the kitchen. It can be quite hard to find relatively untouched ones.

The classic cars of Heartbeat:
▲ Nick Rowan in his beloved MG TA.
▶ Nick and Kate with Kate's trusty Triumph Herald.
▼ Greengrass' pink Chrysler Imperial.

'My job is to spot the right location for any scene. I have been with Yorkshire for twenty years, so I know the area quite well and often have something in mind as soon as I see a script.

'Recently I got permission to use a cottage but only after being frightened half to death. I went and knocked on the door and there was this huge wild man, about 6ft 7in tall, sitting at the kitchen table carving away at a bone with a knife. It was really quite creepy. The farmyard was horrible and there was a carcass just thrown there for the dog to eat. I thought: "My God, what am I doing here. This man is going to drive his knife through me."

'He didn't do that, but he said he wasn't bloody interested and told me to bugger off. Then six months later I was given another episode and I knew this farmhouse would be perfect, so I plucked up my courage and had another go. In the end I talked him round.'

Householders who allow Yorkshire to film on their property do get paid a daily fee which varies according to the amount of use made of the location and the disruption caused to it. The deal is usually that the company will leave any property the way they find it. Therefore any changes made to gain an authentic Sixties look have to be changed back afterwards. The more this has to be done, the more it costs, so the search for locations needing as little 'set dressing' as possible is a vital one.

Even allowing for a little cheating – whether it's houses, clothes or vehicles – the Sixties look of *Heartbeat* is a vital ingredient in its success story.

▼ *To the rest of us it's an old wreck of a car – but to Greengrass it's a perfectly good barn!*

◀ Dr Kate measures out a dose of her medicine.

▶ Ashfordly police station made to look in period-style by the set designers.

BEHIND THE SCENES:
On Location

—

The sleepy moorland village of Goathland will never be the same now that it has become the central location for one of the most popular drama series on television. Several times a day the tourist coaches out of Leeds and Whitby spew their loads on to the wide grassy verges of this village, which was previously known outside the Yorkshire Moors only to the steady stream of hikers passing through. Now they come to see *Heartbeat* being filmed – to beg autographs from Nick Berry and Niamh Cusack and to pick up on some of the reflected glamour which invariably attaches itself to a major TV series.

Goathland's principal source of income has for many years been the tourist industry. The village is a picturesque collection of houses, shops and hostelries set in the heart of the Yorkshire Moors. There are virtually no modern buildings or other new development to get in the way of the film makers and hinder the transformation to *Heartbeat*'s Aidensfield. A few double yellow lines have to be blacked out on the main road but that is about the only alteration necessary.

The local pub, The Goathland Hotel, is renamed The Aidensfield Arms for the duration, and at one time landlord Keith Richardson kept the sign up even after filming halted. He reckoned it was so good for business. 'Anyway they kept breaking it every time they took it down', he says.

Goathland is set on the main line of the North Yorks Steam Railway and has its own delightfully old-fashioned railway station. This was an added attraction

▲ The age of steam. The railway is an important feature of Heartbeat.

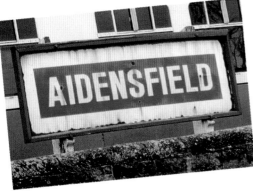

▶ The train crash from Series 3 – one of Heartbeat's most spectacular action sequences.

to the programme-makers, and trains and station have featured frequently in the series. 'I bought an entire railway carriage from the North Yorks Railway when we had the train crash on *Heartbeat*', says production buyer David Eaton. 'We had to smash it up which was a bit of a shame.'

The economy of Goathland has been greatly boosted by *Heartbeat*. Cast and crew rent cottages and stay in the village's two hotels, the Mallyan Spout Hotel and the Inn on the Moor, when they are on location and many local people have been used as extras in the show. Malcolm Simpson, landlord of the Inn on the Moor, reckons he has appeared in a staggering twenty episodes. 'My biggest role was in the episode called "Bang to Rights" in the second series when I played a character called Harry Paxton who beats up PC Bellamy on his stag night', he recalls. 'I was a bit surprised when I got the script because Harry Paxton was described as a burly footballer in his early twenties. I'm a bit burly but I'm in my fifties. Poetic licence, they told me . . . '

That was a speaking role, but most of Malcolm's appearances have been as a silent extra. 'I'm usually an ornament in the pub', he says. 'Whatever I've done I have enjoyed. We've had a lot of fun with the series.'

One role Malcolm has never played in the show is a policeman, which he might have been rather good at. He retired in 1980 as a detective inspector in the Metropolitan Police Force. 'I'd be a bit too rough for Ashfordly. I was a serving policeman in the Sixties, but the Met was a bit different to this lot.

'Mind you, I've seen some Blaketons in my time, and yes I have come across gentle policemen like Nick. They do exist. And there are certainly a lot of Ventresses about in all walks of life. All he ever wants is to be left alone.'

Malcolm has no doubt that *Heartbeat* has been good for Goathland. And over the road at The Goathland Hotel these opinions are shared by Keith Richardson, who by coincidence shares the same name as *Heartbeat*'s executive producer. His pub is so central to the programme that it is taken over totally during the making of each series, and Keith has also been an extra in the show several times.

Accompanied by his thirteen-year-old son, he spent much of one episode walking around a fairground, and in 'Going Home' in the third series he was a bloodthirsty spectator at the bare-knuckle fist fight. 'But I think the best time was when I played a drinker in my own bar, and there I was, also the landlord and also the executive producer', he says. 'It can be a bit confusing, certainly.'

Southerner Keith, from Eastbourne, has been in the catering or pub trade most of his life and has run The Goathland Hotel for nine years. '*Heartbeat* has been great for business, of course', he enthuses. 'Mind you, when Yorkshire first asked if they could film here I had no idea that the series would go on for so long. When they are filming in the pub we have to close the place, but we do usually manage to open in the evenings.

'They liked this pub because on the surface it has not changed much since the Sixties. The front is still the same, and the bar could be a Sixties bar more or less as it stands.'

Unlike some productions there is an easy relationship between crew and spectators in the village. Big crowds gather and wait patiently to catch a glimpse of the stars of the show at work. Polite calls for silence during filming are obeyed to an extraordinary degree. I was once in Goathland when a scene was being filmed inside The Goathland Hotel, in the bar of the fictional Aidensfield Arms. When a unit assistant asked for quiet during shooting there was instant hush and one young man was so anxious to comply that he walked on tip-toe softly down the street away from the action – taking with him his Labrador dog whom he thought was panting too noisily.

By and large almost all the people of Goathland and the surrounding areas welcome the *Heartbeat* crew. They bring life and cash even during the long hard winter months. During filming of the third series the Mallyan Spout Hotel and the village store were able to keep a full staff on all winter for the first time.

'We've always been a tourist village – but not in the winter', says store owner Mrs Veronica Lewis. '*Heartbeat* has definitely been good for Goathland – there is no doubt about it.' She sells everything from sunglasses to sugar, but now *Heartbeat* memorabilia is big business – with T-shirts and pens, postcards, guides to *Heartbeat* country, and souvenir crockery proving popular lines.

When it first became known that Goathland was to be the central *Heartbeat* location some locals were not so sure, fearing that their village would be swamped by the film crew. One even organized a petition against it. Yorkshire TV and the *Heartbeat* crew have, however, made a real effort to operate sensitively alongside the villagers. There is a considerable sense of mutual goodwill.

▲ *William Simons, Nick Berry, Tricia Penrose, Stuart Golland, Mark Jordon, Derek Fowlds and Bill Maynard in the bar of the 'Aidensfield Arms'.*

▶ *(Overleaf) An old traditional scene in an old traditional village. However, AA signs are good examples of the modern features that have to be removed by the set designers or kept carefully out of shot.*

Says producer Martyn Auty: 'I think it helps that the series has kept the same crew. They think of Goathland as their second home.' Location manager Mary Rotherham adds: 'I always feel confident with this crew when I take them into people's homes that they will behave considerately. They are that kind of bunch.'

Other locations used regularly include Otley, where the interior of Dr Ferrenby's old surgery was based, and the village of Askwith, about ten miles out of Leeds, where Nick and Kate's police house can be found. Whitby is the home of *Heartbeat*'s hospital and the location of Kate's new surgery after she teams up with Dr James Radcliffe. In the fourth *Heartbeat* series the seaside town begins to feature more and more.

Wherever the location – and, rare among TV series, *Heartbeat* is shot entirely on location – the back-up required by a film shoot is considerable. They make one episode every ten days and then have a four-day break. But at least one of those four days is taken up in planning for the designers and production team, and in script read-through for the actors. The schedule is tight and demanding. Everything has to work like clockwork. Mistakes made and time wasted cost money and in a project as big as this – fifteen hours of TV to be shot in less than seven months – could destroy the whole enterprise.

It is legend in the business that just as armies march on their stomachs, so do film units. *Heartbeat* has its own caterers, GT Caterers of Leeds, who in the tradition of their specialist trade produce vast meals of an extraordinarily high standard several times a day from the back of a truck – their mobile kitchen. A single-decker bus parked next to the catering truck is the traditional travelling restaurant on film locations – the original bench seating is rearranged on either side of canteen-style fixed tables.

Such is the devotion of British film and TV crews to their favourite caterers that they are frequently hired to drive their catering trucks overland to feed productions on locations worldwide. GT have been all over Europe.

One of the most famous catering stories concerns ITV's celebrated *Jewel in the Crown*, filmed largely on location in India. Cast and crew just could not get on with the local food or caterers, and so in the end a British-based catering truck was sent all the way to India in order to keep the troops going.

On each location a kind of base camp is set up – often in a pub car park. This is where the vehicles transporting crew and cast are parked alongside caravan dressing-rooms for the principal artists. Here Nick, Kate and the rest can change costumes, relax and learn their lines between scenes – and also thaw out a little when the weather is really bad.

In Goathland the *Heartbeat* team set up their own production office in the Inn on the Moor, complete with several direct phones lines and a fax machine. At other locations the production team work on their feet using mobile phones for communication with each other and the TV Centre back in Leeds.

At the time of writing mobile phones still do not work in Goathland, which has virtually no reception at all, and there are those in Yorkshire TV who believe this has always been one of the outstanding reasons for the popularity of Goathland among the crew. However, sad news arrived in the spring of 1994 – mobile phone reception areas were being improved in the area and would soon include the sleepy moorland town.

For production co-ordinator Teresa Ferlinc, based in the Leeds TV Centre, more mobile phones will only make her life easier. In fact, she says: 'I have worked on productions in the days before we all had mobile phones, but it is difficult to imagine now how we managed without them. You get so used to things.' Teresa prints a call sheet for each shooting day which gives location places and call times for artists and crew, and details contact numbers for all concerned.

One of the most important phone numbers on her list is that of the Leeds Weather Centre. Shoots often have to be changed around at the last moment because of bad weather. The daily schedules are worked out by associate producer Pat Brown, and it is up to her to juggle the demands of filming: 'We have ten days for each episode and it doesn't matter what order we film in, but all the scenes have to be completed in that time. Incredibly, and it is something of a miracle, we have yet to drop a scene. We have always completed everything according to the script. But it has been touch and go sometimes.' Pat and Teresa have to ensure that cast and crew know about the changes of plan and where they should be at what time each day.

Almost all of the *Heartbeat* team are Yorkshire TV employees, the experts employed permanently in every sphere of production. But some areas are so specialized that outside help must be drawn in: the use of animals is one of these.

Heartbeat regularly features cats, dogs, pigs and sheep. Animal trainer Sue Beale, whose agency Woofers provides a variety of meticulously trained creatures for film and TV work, is responsible for making sure they do the right thing at the right time – or more or less.

It is Sue who has trained Tramp, Greengrass's Alfred, of whom she says: 'Lurchers are notoriously bad to train, not an easy type at all, and at first Tramp was difficult but he took to it very quickly once he had got over the initial hurdle. He goes wild now when I pick him up to take him on location.

'I think the biggest secret of it is to choose the right animal. It sounds crazy, but some animals are naturals. They take to it easily and seem to enjoy it. I have forty or fifty animals on my books which are available to TV and film companies, and, of course, I do a great deal of work with *Heartbeat*. It has mostly been cats and dogs that I have supplied to them, but I am about to start training some pigs.

'On other programmes I have supplied all sorts of animals. We have a tame fox called Caspar who has yet to appear in *Heartbeat* but could fit into all kinds of storylines with Greengrass. He was found with a broken leg when he was four weeks-old and brought up among domestic dogs. He was too lame to ever let go and now he lives just like a dog. They say foxes will never be tame, but this one is.'

Probably the strangest animal Sue ever trained for a TV programme was a frog. 'It was for a children's programme and the frog had to sit on a presenter's hand and then jump on cue on to a lily leaf in a pond and stay there', she recalls. 'He

▶ Huddled up
against the cold,
director and crew
set up a shot.
▲ Niamh outside
Kate's surgery on
a warmer day.
▼ Cast and crew
use golf umbrellas
against the rain.

also had to jump out of a teapot. And he did it too. I trained him the same way I train all animals – by signal and reward. You give them titbits all the time – in the frog's case nice juicy flies. It calls for a lot of patience – that is the other secret.'

The third series of *Heartbeat* included an episode in which badger baiters came to Aidensfield. This is a real-life problem so prevalent in country areas that badger protection people are inclined to be very secretive about the animals' whereabouts. Even Sue Beale could not help buyer Dave Eaton, who has over-all responsibility for acquiring the animals as well as the objects needed on set. He tells how he had to go further afield: 'I had to speak to a lot of people very nicely before they would trust me with their secrets. In the end we were taken to film all the badgers we needed. But we had to go to them and we swore to keep the secret of where they actually were.'

The North Yorks Moors, where so much of *Heartbeat* is filmed, form a 553 square mile National Park. Its raw beauty and architectural heritage – it boasts some of the finest examples of religious architecture in Britain, notably Whitby Abbey – have enhanced the appeal of the series. Yorkshire TV are convinced that, like *All Creatures Great and Small* before it, viewers, particularly those abroad, switch on for the stunning scenery almost as much as the stories and the stars.

The locations of *Heartbeat* and its supporting cast of locals – human and animal – are of vital importance to the show. And the machine which keeps the whole operation running smoothly is a formidable one.

▼ *Animal scenes are the hardest of all to get right. Here, Greengrass and a herd of sheep cause chaos for Blaketon.*

HEARTBEAT:

CHAPTER AND VERSE

THE SIXTIES SOUND OF *HEARTBEAT*

The extensive use of Sixties hits in *Heartbeat* started as an accident, as explained by executive producer Keith Richardson. What began with music of the time being played on people's radios during certain scenes, became a sound which grew and grew.

Nowadays, the sound of *Heartbeat* is certainly no accident. The songs and tunes used are meticulously chosen and adapted where necessary by a specialist team, headed by Adrian Burch and David Whitaker – *Heartbeat*'s musician researchers and librarians. Adrian and David are also composers and performers. They write most of the incidental music used in the show themselves and perform much of it on synthesizers, guitars, and other instruments. They also play a part in choosing and unearthing the Sixties originals played. Before working on *Heartbeat* Adrian, 30, remembered listening to Sixties music on the radio as a kid, but had little knowledge. Now he is something of an expert.

'Sometimes the directors choose songs and sometimes we do', he says. 'We use the music in three ways. We use it as background, we feature it – like when someone actually plays the radio or a record in a scene or one of the cast sings a song – and we use it as a method of getting the characters from A to B. If Nick is going on a journey on his bike we play a record to get him to his destination.'

Yorkshire TV pay a fee every year to the Musicians' Copyright Protection Society for the rights to use original musical recordings. Nonetheless, sometimes there are complications, and particularly when *Heartbeat* is sold abroad there are often different deals on the table in different countries. Session musicians are then sometimes dubbed over the original artist to comply with regulations.

In Britain the programme uses mostly hit recordings performed by the original artists, but when clearance can not be acquired, session musicians or lesser known recordings are used. In addition to Nick Berry's re-recording of the Buddy Holly hit, 'Heartbeat', as the theme tune of the series, some songs are sung by members of the *Heartbeat* cast as part of an episode's storyline as in 'A Talent for Deception', when Tricia Penrose sang a version of Lulu's hit, 'Shout'.

The Hits of *Heartbeat*

■ As well as the storylines of each episode, this chapter provides a guide to the songs of *Heartbeat* including when they became hit records – almost always in the Sixties. The date given is the date they entered the *New Musical Express* Top Thirty Charts. Some numbers, particularly by the Beatles, were not charted single hits but were recorded on albums, almost all in the Sixties. And although most of the single records used on *Heartbeat* were hits, some, despite being popular songs, did not quite make it.

Series 1

Episode 1:
'Changing Places'
Writer – Johnny Byrne
Director – Roger Cheveley

■ London policeman Nick Rowan and his recently qualified doctor wife Kate decide to quit the city and head north to the little village of Aidensfield in moorland Yorkshire where Kate was born.

The Rowans are outsiders who have to prove themselves before being accepted into the community, and Nick's new boss, Station Sergeant Blaketon, is not too sure about his recruit from the smoke: 'You're not one of these young constables with the wrong attitude, I hope, Rowan? If you've come up north looking for a cushy number . . .'

Nonetheless PC Rowan becomes Aidensfield's village bobby. Aidensfield's police house is now home. And as Blaketon acidly tells Kate on their first meeting: 'If he's here, he's on duty.'

Nick and Kate may have left behind the rapes, robberies, muggings and murder of the metropolis, but they find themselves occupied twenty-four hours a day with the trials and tribulations of village life.

Any dreams they may have of rural tranquillity are destroyed on arrival when a group of local motorcycle rockers 'buzz' the Rowans' Triumph Herald.

Nick is then confronted with one of Aidensfield's most colourful characters, Claude Jeremiah Greengrass, whose dog, Alfred, breaks into an aviary and kills a budgie. Blaketon insists that Nick charge him with livestock worrying, but, in a masterly courtroom appearance before the magistrates, Greengrass points out that, within the meaning of the act, budgies are not livestock. He walks free.

Nick also investigates a mystery prowler allegedly terrorizing a prim and proper lady resident, and evicts a gang of 'mods' intent on making trouble at the village hall hop.

Kate also faces problems. Dr Ferrenby, the old-fashioned, chain-smoking local GP who had half-promised her a job in his practice, withdraws the offer – and

▼ *The village hall hop: bopping to the sound of the Sixties.*

admits to an angry Kate that the reason is mainly because she is a woman. But Kate is called in when Mrs Maskell is giving birth, and saves the baby.

It is not an easy beginning, yet Nick and Kate are determined to make their new way of life work.

> 'Always Something There to Remind Me', **Sandie Shaw** (10.10.64)
> 'Stranger on the Shore', **Mr Acker Bilk** (2.12.61)
> 'Boom Boom', **Animals** (album track)
> 'Do You Love Me?', sung on the show by actors in a group called **Telstars** specially formed for *Heartbeat* from the Brian Poole and the Tremeloes hit (14.9.63)
> 'Twist and Shout', as above (6.7.63)
> 'Tutti Frutti', sung by **Telstars** from the Little Richard hit (23.2.57)
> 'Hippy Hippy Shake', sung by **Telstars** from the Swinging Blue Jeans hit (28.12.63)

Episode 2:
'Fruits of the Earth'
Writer – Johnny Byrne
Director – Tim Dowd

■ Nick is perplexed by a succession of drunken hikers, one of whom is responsible for an accident in which a ram is killed. He cautions Potter, a man with one arm, for passing on illicit liquor – home-made wine. Potter also finds himself accused of indecent exposure, but it turns out that the stump of his second arm has been the subject of mistaken identity . . .

An employee at the bank reports her husband missing, and Nick learns that she is having an affair with the bank manager. Her husband is found to have hanged himself. When Alan Maskell is refused a bank loan Nick is able to use this tragedy to persuade the manager to change his mind.

Kate has further trouble with Dr Ferrenby. While visiting the Maskell family to check on the new baby she realizes that mother-of-six Susan Maskell is nearing the end of her tether and suggests that Susan should take the contraceptive pill. Ferrenby is opposed, and Susan's husband sees it as a threat to his virility. Against the odds, Kate wins both men round.

> 'All Day and All of the Night', **Kinks** (31.10.64)
> 'Hippy Hippy Shake', **Swinging Blue Jeans** (28.12.63)
> 'A Picture of You', **Joe Brown** (19.5.62)
> 'You Really Got Me', **Kinks** (15.8.64)
> 'My Boy Lollipop', **Millie** (21.3.64; rereleased and re-entered the charts 15.8.87)

Episode 3:
'Rumours'
Writer – David Lane
Director – Ken Horn

■ PC Rowan finds himself investigating a malicious whispering campaign against village shopkeeper Charlie Denby whose record department is a popular hang-out for the local teenage lads.

Nick receives an anonymous letter accusing Denby of taking 'an unhealthy interest in young boys' and discovers that there have also been anonymous phone-calls to the station.

Nick investigates and can find no evidence of any such behaviour. But the vendetta continues. Denby is driven out of the local Masons and dies in a car accident, probably caused by strain on his dicky heart. The chief rumour-monger turns out to be Denby's secret half-brother.

Spinster sisters René and Frances Kirby move into Laburnum Cottage with some expensive looking antique furniture. They advertise for a gardener. Greengrass, seeing an opportunity for some fast and easy money, applies and cons the

▲ *Greengrass thinks he can get the better of René and Frances Kirby (Elizabeth Spriggs and Judith Davis), but they prove more than a match for him.*

93

sisters into selling him valuable antiques for a fraction of their value – or so he thinks. In fact the 'antiques' turn out to be worthless.

'House of the Rising Sun', **Animals** (27.6.64; rereleased and re-entered the charts 7.10.72 and 9.10.82)
'A Hard Day's Night', **Beatles** (18.7.64)
'I Like It', **Gerry and the Pacemakers** (1.6.63)
'Don't Let the Sun Catch You Crying', **Gerry and the Pacemakers** (18.4.64)
'I'm Into Something Good', **Herman's Hermits** (29.8.64)
'Shout', **Lulu and the Lovers** (16.5.64; rereleased and re-entered the charts 2.8.86)
'Bits and Pieces', **Dave Clark Five** (22.2.64)
'Needles and Pins', **Searchers** (18.1.64)

Episode 4:
'Playing with Fire'
Writer – Rob Gittins
Director – Eric Wendell

■ Nick investigates two mysterious barn fires and tracks down the arsonist who turns out to be a youth with a sexual problem. He also has to remonstrate with the owner of a runaway horse which keeps escaping from its field and destroys a sentimentally priceless garden statue. Apart from the damage, Nick is concerned that the animal could cause a road accident.

He has another animal case to deal with. Greengrass gives him a tip-off that a salmon poaching gang has moved into the area and a police operation to trap them is launched. But the police have been tricked. A bigger gang clear the river at a different spot.

Kate has another run in with Dr Ferrenby, over birth control. She advises an unmarried woman to go to a family planning clinic and Ferrenby is incensed.

'Good Golly Miss Molly', **Swinging Blue Jeans** (2.3.64)
'Help!', **Beatles** (31.7.65)
'You're No Good', **Swinging Blue Jeans** (6.6.64)
'If You Gotta Make a Fool of Somebody', **Freddie and the Dreamers** (18.5.63)
'A World Without Love', **Peter and Gordon** (21.3.64)
'I Believe', **Bachelors** (21.3.64)
'Do You Want to Know a Secret?', **Billy J. Kramer and the Dakotas** (4.5.63)
'Ramona', **Bachelors** (6.6.64)
'Tell Me When', **Applejacks** (14.3.64)

Episode 5:
Nowt but a Prank
Writer – Barry Woodward
Director – James Ormerod

■ A twenty-year-old feud between two Aidensfield neighbours erupts into full-scale warfare. Teenage lads play a series of nasty pranks on local farmer Matthew Chapman who automatically blames his neighbour and old enemy, Radcliffe, and cuts off the right of way to Radcliffe's home. Ferrenby is called out to visit Radcliffe who is diabetic. The doctor is met by a shotgun-wielding Chapman and falls while trying to shift barbed wire barring his path. He is forced to ask Kate to help with his practice.

Chapman takes Radcliffe prisoner and when Nick intervenes he is also threatened with a shotgun and locked up with Radcliffe. Nick escapes and summons the rest of the police and Kate, who discovers that the reclusive Mrs Radcliffe had been engaged to Chapman before the war but had married when he was taken prisoner and went missing presumed dead.

Ferrenby asks Kate if she would like to formally join his practice. She asks for time to think.

▌'I Can't Explain', **Who** (21.2.65)
'Hello Little Girl', **Fourmost** (21.9.63)
'When You Walk in the Room', **Searchers** (19.9.64)
'I'm Telling You Now', **Freddie and the Dreamers** (10.8.63)
'Diamonds', **Jet Harris/Tony Meehan** (12.1.63)

▼ *At each other's throats: local farmers Chapman (James Cosmos) and Radcliffe (Paul Copley) face up to each other.*

95

Episode 6:
'Old, New, Borrowed and Blue'
Writer – Alan Whiting
Director – Tim Dowd

■ Alan Maskell and Sandra Murray get married. Nick and Kate are invited to the wedding, but Nick ends up arresting the best man for pushing drugs. Nick also investigates the case of a house-proud housebreaker who has a fetish for tidying up. They catch him when he burgles Lord Ashfordly's home and straightens a picture which is wired to the police station.

Meanwhile Nick is becoming suspicious of a local do-gooder, who looks after elderly sick people with no relatives. He believes the woman steals antique objects – always one of a set – from her dying charges, and when their effects are disposed of, usually at auction, buys the incomplete set for a fraction of its true value and sells it on complete. Although he cannot prove the charge, the woman leaves the area.

Kate is considering returning to hospital medicine. None the less she goes on rounds with Ferrenby, and although this highlights their occasional differing attitudes, she agrees to join him as a partner.

▼ All smiles, but Nick ends up unsure of local do-gooder Penelope Stirling (Annette Crosbie).

'Green Onions', **Georgie Fame** (uncharted)
'Applejack', **Jet Harris/Tony Meehan** (7.9.63)
'Nut Rocker', **B. Bumble and the Stingers** (14.4.62)
'A Groovy Kind of Love', **Mindbenders** (22.1.66)
'A Walk in the Black Forest', **Russ Conway** (uncharted)

Episode 7:
'Face Value'
Writer – David Lane
Director – Terry Iland

▲ *Prospective
MP Paul Melthorn
(John Duttine) is a
man with a past.*

■ There is to be a CND demonstration outside Fylingdales, the newly opened American-run early warning defence system on the outskirts of Aidensfield, at which left-wing parliamentary candidate Paul Melthorn is to speak. Preparations lead to ugly incidents. Nick finds himself accused of assault on one of the demonstrators, a Melthorn sidekick.

A construction worker and his friend, Billy, burgle the demonstrators' campsite and steal Melthorn's wallet which contains incriminating photographs detailing his affair with a young student. The burglary ends in a scuffle and Billy's arm is broken. He fakes an accident at work in order to secure medical treatment – given by Kate who tells Nick about it.

⸙ The Melthorn sidekick turns out to be a Special Branch officer investigating Melthorn's love life. However, Nick and Blaketon decide to return the incriminating wallet to Melthorn on condition that he calls the demonstration off.

'*Needles and Pins*', **Searchers** (18.1.64)
'*Goodness Gracious Me*', **Peter Sellers and Sophia Loren** (12.11.60)
'*I Saw Her Standing There*', **Beatles** (album)
'*I'm Telling You Now*', **Freddie and the Dreamers** (10.8.63)
'*Little Things*', **Dave Berry** (27.3.65)
'*You Can't Do That*', **Beatles** (album)
'*Twist and Shout*', **Beatles** (20.7.63)

Episode 8:
'Outsiders'
Writer – Peter Barwood
Director – Tim Dowd

■ A caravan of circus-folk, the Laszlos, arrive in the village and camp on the green, to the dismay of the locals. Vicar's daughter Anna falls heavily for handsome Milos Laszlo, to the fury of wealthy farmer's son Jamie Hunter to whom she is engaged. Amidst allegations of trespassing and theft, Nick visits the caravan and discovers that there is a sick man inside, but he is not allowed to see him.

He then halts a fight between Milos and Jamie but agrees not to press charges on condition that Kate can visit the sick man. She discovers he is a one-time local suffering from cancer who wanted to return to Aidensfield to die.

Bitterness against the Laszlos grows after an outbreak of petty crime. Jamie's MG is vandalized and the stolen toolbox found at the caravan. The church safe is broken into, and Milos's scarf found at the scene of the crime. Things look bad for Milos but the scarf turns out to have been planted by Jamie – and the caravan moves on with a new recruit, Anna.

'*Little Children*', **Billy J. Kramer and the Dakotas** (29.2.64)
'*I Think of You*', **Merseybeats** (18.1.64)
'*A Hard Day's Night*', **Beatles** (18.7.64)
'*I Feel Fine*', **Beatles** (5.12.64)
'*Secret Love*', **Kathy Kirby** (9.11.63)
'*Everything's Alright*', **Mojos** (11.4.64)
'*The Crying Game*', **Dave Berry** (22.8.64)

▼ *Tempers run high when the gypsy Laszlos arrive in Aidensfield.*

Episode 9:
'Primal Instinct'
Writer – Brian Finch
Director – Ken Horn

▲ *Murder in the village – with both Nick and Kate on duty.*

■ Aidensfield becomes the scene of a murder hunt when a top London copper is shot dead. Andrew Gerard, a former senior detective with Scotland Yard, is murdered one Sunday morning and two London policemen are sent to the village to investigate. One of them, DC Langton, is an old friend of Nick's; Kate invites him to stay but is outraged when he turns amorous.

The investigation concentrates on the theory that Gerard was killed by an old criminal adversary until Nick discovers from Ferrenby, via Kate, that Gerard had been a wife beater.

Suspicion then shifts to Mrs Gerard, who had allegedly found her husband's body after returning from church with her mother. In fact the culprit turns out to have been her mother.

Alan Maskell gets caught up in a stolen-car racket through no fault of his own – he does a respray job on a car which turns out to be stolen. He tells the police and the thieves are arrested, but Blaketon, much to Nick's dismay, says the law must take its course and insists on charging Alan as well.

'*Norwegian Wood*', **Beatles** (album)
'*Keep on Running*', **Spencer Davis Group** (11.12.65)
'*The Times They Are A-Changin'*', Session musician **Nick Moran** from the Bob Dylan hit (27.3.65)
'*A Whiter Shade of Pale*', **Procol Harum** (27.5.67)
'*Out of Time*', **Chris Farlowe** (2.7.66)
'*The Look of Love*', **Dusty Springfield** (uncharted)
'*Living in the Past*', **Jethro Tull** (31.5.69)

▼ *Farmer Huggett (Peter Armitage) tells Nick as soon as he suspects that Greengrass has taken his sheep.*

Episode 10:
'Keep on Running'
Writer – Johnny Byrne
Director – Gavin Theoditis

■ There is an outbreak of sheep-rustling and one of the victims, renowned for knowing all of his sheep by sight and name, accuses Greengrass of possessing some of his stolen flock. Greengrass ends up in court and is convicted, but Nick discovers discrepancies in the evidence.

Alan Maskell is released on bail and does a runner to London. Nick is head-hunted to join a drugs team at Scotland Yard – promotion to sergeant guaranteed. He decides to go to London for the interview even though Kate, to his surprise, is violently opposed to the idea of returning to the city.

Nick agrees to try to find Alan Maskell while he is in London and tracks him down to a dubious club. There is a drugs bust during which drugs are planted by police. Nick is arrested along with everybody else and files an official complaint. He is told by his prospective boss at the Yard that he must not rock the boat and should withdraw his complaint.

Nick remembers why he left London in the first place and decides to stay in Aidensfield.

> 'Apache', **Shadows** (23.7.60)
> 'Do You Love Me?', **Dave Clark Five** (28.9.63)
> 'If I Fell', **Beatles** (album)
> 'Shakin' All Over', **Johnny Kidd and the Pirates** (25.6.60)
> 'She's Not There', **Zombies** (22.8.64)

Series 2

Episode 1:
'Secrets'
Writer – Adele Rose
Director – Bob Mahoney

■ Back in Aidensfield the rural dramas continue with a highway robbery in which a market trader's van is hijacked and stolen.

Meanwhile Kate starts a mothers and babies group and inadvertently encourages a chicken-pox epidemic.

A village girl becomes pregnant but refuses to name the father. The chief suspect is Rupert, son of Lord Ashfordly, who also becomes a suspect in the hijack

101

case when the empty van is found on the edge of the Ashfordly estate.

Nick is not convinced and investigates further. He identifies the true criminal, Lord Ashfordly's new chauffeur, who also turns out to be the mystery father. The man is well known to the police in London where he has a wife and children.

'I'm the Urban Spaceman', **Bonzo Dog Doo-dah Band** (6.11.68)
'Money', **Beatles** (album)
'Wild Thing', **Troggs** (7.5.66)
'First Cut is the Deepest', **P. P. Arnold** (uncharted)
'Strange Brew', **Cream** (17.6.67)
'My Generation', **Who** (6.11.65)
'Tired of Waiting for You', **Kinks** (23.1.65)
'Lazy Sunday', **Small Faces** (13.4.68)

Episode 2:
'End of the Line'
Writer – David Martin
Director – Bob Mahoney

■ Nick buys an old MG sports car which Greengrass finds in a barn he has been employed to clear. Kate is furious when she learns Nick has bought an old wreck; Greengrass is furious when he learns the potential value of the car.

An elderly widower arrives from London and books into the boarding house opposite the police station. His suitcase contains a Luger pistol. It turns out that he has an old grudge against Nick and has come to Aidensfield seeking revenge. He takes Kate hostage but is unable to carry it through.

'She's Leaving Home', **Beatles** (album)
'Fool on the Hill', **Beatles** (double EP, Magical Mystery Tour 16.12.67)
'Love', **John Lennon** (20.11.82)
'World', **Bee Gees** (25.11.82)
'He Ain't Heavy He's My Brother', **Hollies** (11.10.69; rereleased and re-entered the charts 3.9.88)

Episode 3:
'Manhunt'
Writer – David Lane
Director – Ken Horn

■ Nick interrupts an armed robbery at The Aidensfield Arms. He is knocked out and taken hostage by someone wearing a boiler suit and a balaclava. He ends up locked in the pub cellar for the night with Greengrass.

Information supplied by a drunken Greengrass leads Nick to suspect a local man with a record of armed robbery – but it turns out that the man is dead.

Nick discovers that his suspect had a heart attack during another recent robbery and was dumped on his doorstep by his accomplices. In order to claim National Assistance his wife and daughters had concealed his death and buried him in the garden. They then decided to continue the dead man's career – and his widow had led a series of robberies including the pub raid in which Nick was injured.

'Go Now', **Moody Blues** (19.12.64)
'I Only Wanna Be With You', **Dusty Springfield** (23.11.63)
'Under My Thumb', **Mark Jordon** from the Rolling Stones hit.
'Gimme Some Loving', **Spencer Davis Group** (5.11.66)
'For Miss Caulker', **Animals** (album)
'On a Carousel', **Hollies** (18.2.67)
'Look Through Any Window', **Hollies** (4.9.65)
'Long Live Love', uncharted recording by **Nick Berry** of a
Sandie Shaw hit (15.5.65)

▲ A trio with something to hide: Nell Robinson (Rachel Davies) and her two daughters, Jean and Susan (Anastasia Mulrooney and Samantha Beckinsale), know where the body is buried. . .

Episode 4:
'Bitter Harvest'
Writer – Jane Hollowood
Director – Ken Horn

■ Nick has to take charge during an outbreak of foot and mouth. A sick cow belonging to a local farmer is diagnosed as having the disease.

The police have to notify the Ministry and see that strict quarantine regulations are observed. When the slaughtermen arrive there is a confrontation. The farmer stands at his gate with a shotgun and refuses to let them in.

Nick steps in and talks to the farmer, persuading him that he has no alternative. But the man is so distressed by the destruction of his herd that he shoots himself. The loss was just too much to take.

▼ An upset and angry man: Farmer Reg Manston (James Hazeldine) bars entry to his farm.

'Roadrunner', **Animals** (album)
'Nights in White Satin', **Moody Blues** (20.1.68)
'Do Wah Diddy Diddy', **Manfred Mann** (18.7.64)

Episode 5:
'Over the Hill'
Writer – Johnny Byrne
Director – Tim Dowd

■ An army deserter, a frightened squaddie who mistakenly thinks he has caused the death of a bullying sergeant, is trying to contact an old friend in Aidensfield. The friend has died and Kate is treating his widow whose son, seriously disturbed by the death of his father, may have to be taken into care.

Nick discovers what is happening and prevents the deserter making his situation any worse. And Kate discovers the widow has a barnful of elaborate carvings made by her late husband, which, if sold, could raise enough money to provide properly for mother and boy and help keep the little family together.

Kate also learns of Gina's criminal past – she is on probation and a condition was that she had to leave Liverpool and live quietly in the country.

| 'Hey Joe', **Jimi Hendrix Experience** (14.1.67)
| 'For the Benefit of Mr Kite', **Beatles** (album)
| 'What Do You Want?', **Adam Faith** (21.11.59)

▲ *Army deserter Ken Marston (Roland Gift) carries the son of his dead friend, Daniel (Adam Walsh), to safety after a climbing accident.*

105

Episode 6:
'Bang to Rights'
Writer – Brian Finch
Director – Tim Dowd

■ A habitual thief known as Non-Stick Terry, because the police could never catch him, may have been fitted up by Nick's predecessor in Aidensfield. Nick investigates and finds the policeman had retired unexpectedly. Blaketon warns Nick off, telling him the man retired because he had cancer. Nick, worried that Blaketon may have connived in a cover up, persists. The retired copper finally confesses to framing Non-Stick Terry out of sheer frustration.

Bellamy is about to marry his pregnant girlfriend but at the eleventh hour she tells him she is not pregnant after all. Later she is found in bed with an ex-boyfriend who has already beaten Bellamy up at his stag night.

'Lady D'Arbanville', **Cat Stevens** (11.7.70)
'When You Walk in the Room', **Searchers** (19.9.64)
'Don't Throw Your Love Away', **Searchers** (18.4.64)
'Little Children', **Billy J. Kramer and the Dakotas** (29.2.64)
'Good Golly Miss Molly', **Swinging Blue Jeans** (21.3.64)
'Hippy Hippy Shake', sung by extras in The Aidensfield Arms, from the Swinging Blue Jeans hit (28.12.63)
'You've Got Your Troubles', **Fortunes** (10.7.65)

▼ Nick and Bellamy at his stag night: both unaware of the trouble about to befall the groom-to-be.

•
HEARTBEAT:
CHAPTER AND
VERSE

Episode 7:
'A Talent for Deception'
Writer – Jonathan Critchley
Director – Terry Marcel

▲ *Missing crime writer Amanda Young (Dorothy Tutin) turns up in Aidensfield, causing a mystery of her own.*

■ Nick and Kate fall out when a former boyfriend of hers visits the village and becomes the prime suspect in a hit-and-run incident. Ironically Nick has to tell him not to leave the area. The case is solved when Bellamy organizes a talent contest on behalf of his football team and Nick finds that the true hit-and-run criminal is Bellamy's rival on the football field. Meanwhile, Nick and Bellamy investigate reports of a woman who has been observing the local bank for some time.

Kate, one of the contest judges, realizes that Greengrass is running a book and ensures that his betting activities backfire on him and that he loses a lot of money. However, Greengrass makes a small fortune selling a patch of worthless

107

moorland to the Ministry of Defence and buys a big flash American car.

The mysterious woman who appears to have been planning a robbery turns out to be a woman crime-writer who has been researching for her next book.

> 'What's New Pussycat?', **Tom Jones** (14.8.65)
> 'I'll Never Find Another You', **Billy Fury** (23.1.61)
> 'Bad Boy', **Marty Wilde** (12.12.59)
> 'Ticket to Ride', **Beatles** (17.4.65)
> 'Simon Smith and his Amazing Dancing Bear', **Alan Price** (11.3.67)
> 'Shout', sung by **Tricia Penrose** from Lulu's hit (6.5.64)

Episode 8:
'Baby Blues'
Writer – Veronica Henry
Director – Catherine Morshead

■ Kate is treating a woman driven to despair by her apparent inability to conceive. The woman 'borrows' a baby from a young couple Nick knows because he is frequently called to their domestic disputes. A manhunt is launched for the snatched baby and Kate realizes her patient is probably involved. The baby is returned – via some hippies who have moved into the area in an attempt to get back to nature.

Greengrass buys a racehorse and Nick and Blaketon fight to prevent him training the animal through Aidensfield's main street. But Greengrass has done his homework and knows the by-laws. Nick resorts to lateral thinking and nobbles the jockey.

> 'Hi Ho Silver Lining', **Jeff Beck** (16.4.67)
> 'Colours', **Donovan** (5.6.65)
> 'Catch the Wind', **Donovan** (20.3.65)
> 'Badge', **Cream** (26.4.69)
> 'I've Got That Feeling', **Kinks** (uncharted)
> 'Need Your Love So Bad', **Fleetwood Mac** (16.7.68)

Episode 9:
'Wall of Silence'
Writer – Jane Hollowood
Director – Terry Marcel

■ Lord Ashfordly's winter pheasant shoot is seriously disrupted when the entire contents of the game larder are stolen. A number of petty thefts have been carried out and when Nick investigates he discovers that an unpleasant story of incest lies behind them.

*▲ Chris
Rawlings (Hugo
Speer) and Susan
Rawlings (Rachel
Robertson): a
brother and sister
with a guilty
secret.*

Susan, the daughter of Rawlings, Ashfordly's head keeper, is pregnant and steals £50 from Greengrass's hidden cash hoard in order to pay for an illegal abortion.

Unaware of this, her brother Chris has stolen the pheasants in order to raise cash for the same purpose. He has a guilty secret: he is the father of Susan's unborn child. But she will not give evidence against him.

▌ *'Hey Jude'*, **Beatles** (7.9.68)
▌ *'If I Fell'*, **Beatles** (album)

Episode 10:
'Missing'
Writer – Adele Rose
Director – Terry Marcel

■ The fair comes to town to be greeted with complaints from Edna Plummer who runs a caravan site. But it turns out that her caravan park is used as a convenient meeting place by her criminal brother. He is preparing to collect some stolen works of art from amateur smuggler Norman Currie who has stopped off at the site with his family on his way home from a trip to Holland.

Currie's son takes a valuable painting and barters with it at the fair for free

▲ *Nick and Kate at the fair – but their fun is not allowed to last for long.*

rides. Fairground staff sell the painting to Greengrass who tries to sell it to Ferrenby who recognizes its value and tells Nick.

Meanwhile the Curries' second son, aged five, and another five-year-old each go missing for several hours and return unharmed. Kate realizes that the children's mysterious 'friend' is a young man whose wife and child were recently killed in an accident.

'Yellow Submarine', **Beatles** (13.8.66)
'Matthew and Son', **Cat Stevens** (14.1.67)
'Alfie', **Cilla Black** (2.4.66)
'A Picture of You', **Joe Brown** (19.5.62)
'Let the Heartaches Begin', **Long John Baldry** (11.11.67)
'Secret Love', **Kathy Kirby** (9.11.63)
'Mighty Quinn', **Manfred Mann** (20.1.68)
'What Becomes of the Broken Hearted?', **Chris Farlowe** (uncharted)
'High in the Sky', **Amen Corner** (10.8.68)
'Bend Me Shape Me', **Amen Corner** (27.1.68)

Series 3

Episode 1:
'Speed Kills'
Writer – David Martin
Director – Terry Marcel

■ There is a break-in at the surgery and Ferrenby is hit over the head. He is taken to hospital where he is a terrible patient. Stolen pills are passed off as speed and other drugs, and a friend of Gina's ends up in a coma. Nick identifies the pushers, who have stolen Greengrass's American car. In the course of making the arrest a fire is started in their workshop which badly burns one of the pushers and destroys Greengrass's car.

◀ *Fire in a makeshift drugs factory.* ▼ *Nick and Bellamy finally apprehend the dealers, but it was a near thing for Nick.*

111

Kate finds out that a patient's miscarriages have been caused by some German drugs she was taking for morning sickness.

Nick learns of the softer side of Blaketon. The sergeant has an eighteen-year-old son whom he only sees at school football matches, and he has compensated for his lost family by adopting the children's ward at the local hospital where he is a regular visitor.

'Simon Smith and his Amazing Dancing Bear', **Alan Price** (11.3.67)
'FBI', **The Shadows** (album)
'House of the Rising Sun', **The Animals** (27.6.64; rereleased and re-entered the charts 7.10.72 and 9.10.82)
'My Boy Lollipop', **Millie** (21.3.64)
'Fried Onions', **Lord Rockingham's XI** (uncharted)
'The Crying Game', **Dave Berry** (22.8.64)
'Itchycoo Park', **Small Faces** (19.8.67)
'Don't Bring Me Down', **Pretty Things** (31.10.64)

Episode 2:
'Riders of the Storm'
Writer – Brian Finch
Director – Tim Dowd

■ Aidensfield is cut off in a snowstorm. There is a train crash, the power lines are down and a pregnant woman stranded in an isolated cottage is about to give birth. On top of all of that an ex-convict returns to the village to retrieve his ill-gotten gains – and the pregnant woman, who now lives with her boyfriend, is his wife.

Nick hears from Blaketon that all roads are cut, the authorities are bringing up an emergency train with a snowplough, but Nick alone will have to deal with the crisis for some hours.

The villagers turn out in full force and bring the injured passengers from the crashed train to the village hall where a generator supplied by Greengrass is fixed by the ex-con, who then sets off in a tractor, ostensibly to rescue his wife and her boyfriend – and Kate who is stranded with them. But his real motive, it turns out, is to clear the way to recover the proceeds of his last robbery from its hiding place in the cottage.

'Time Has Told Me', **Nick Drake** (uncharted)
'Magical Mystery Tour', **The Beatles** (16.12.67)
'Get Away', **Georgie Fame** (26.6.66)
'Crossroads', **Cream** (album)
'Paint It Black', **Chris Farlowe** from the Rolling Stones hit (21.5.66)
'Crosstown Traffic', **Jimi Hendrix Experience** (12.4.69)

◀ *Nick checks
on Dr Ferrenby
when he is injured
in a train crash
during a
snowstorm.*

Episode 3:
'Dead Ringer'
Writer – Johnny Byrne
Director – Tim Dowd

■ A pawnbroker in Ashfordly is broken into one night when Bellamy should have been in the area. Following a tip-off Nick finds stolen goods stashed in a lock-up rented in Bellamy's name. Nick realizes that someone is trying to fit up his colleague but Bellamy is suspended pending inquiries.

Greengrass gets involved in a complex betting scam which entails substituting one greyhound for another. A local underworld character called Scarman is the instigator of this plan. And Nick discovers that Bellamy has been seeing a local girl who turns out to be Scarman's girlfriend.

Nick cannot prove that Scarman set up Bellamy in revenge, but there is enough circumstantial evidence to let the policeman off the hook, and Scarman's girlfriend confirms that she was with Bellamy on the night of the burglary.

'*The Wind Cries Mary*', **Jimi Hendrix Experience** (13.5.67)
'*Jollity Farm*', **Bonzo Dog Doo-Dah Band** (uncharted)
'*She's Not There*', **Zombies** (22.8.64)
'*Do You Love Me?*', **Brian Poole and the Tremeloes** (14.9.63)
'*Mr Slater's Parrot*', **Bonzo Dog Doo-Dah Band** (uncharted)
'*You're No Good*', **Swinging Blue Jeans** (1.6.64)
'*You've Got Your Troubles*', **Fortunes** (10.7.65)

113

Episode 4:
'Going Home'
Writer – Johnny Byrne
Director – Bob Mahoney

■ Ferrenby dies. He becomes disorientated while fishing and drowns. We later learn he has been suffering from a slow brain haemorrhage, probably brought on by the head injury he suffered in the burglary.

A German American visitor to Aidensfield attacks a local landowner intending to kill him but cannot go through with it. The man is arrested and Nick is assigned to escort him back to the area. He learns that the landowner had been an SS traitor during the war and was responsible for the visitor and his family being sent to Nazi concentration camps.

Greengrass helps some gypsies organize a bout of bare-fist fighting, which Nick and Blaketon put a stop to, but cannot prove Greengrass's involvement.

'Baba O'Riley', **Who** (album)
'Oh Well – Part 1', **Fleetwood Mac** (11.10.69)
'Something in the Air', **Thunderclap Newman** (21.6.69)
'Paper Sun', **Traffic** (10.6.67)
'Windmills of Your Mind', **Noel Harrison** (8.3.69)
'Just Like a Woman', **Joe Cocker** uncharted version of the Manfred Mann hit (13.8.66)
'The Good, The Bad, and The Ugly', **Hugo Montenegro** (5.10.68)
'Let It Be', **Joe Cocker** uncharted version of the Beatles hit (14.3.70)

▼ *A man with a deadly mission: German-American visitor, Victor Kellerman (Clive Swift).*

Episode 5:
'A Chilly Reception'
Writer – Eric Wendell
Director – Catherine Morshead

▲ *Kate's aunt Eileen (Anne Stallybrass) brings her a legacy and some bad memories.*

■ A local wedding appears to be sabotaged, possibly by the bride to be. Nick and Kate investigate and find that the culprit is the bride's former boyfriend. An old friend of Greengrass uses him to pass on a load of stolen food which gives the bride's father food poisoning.

An aunt of Kate's pays a visit bringing a legacy from Kate's uncle which she initially refuses, puzzling Nick. It transpires that Kate once found her uncle in bed with another woman and he tried to bribe her not to tell her aunt. When her aunt reveals that she was aware of her husband's womanizing, Kate accepts the money and gives it to charity in memory of Ferrenby.

'*Don't Throw Your Love Away*', **Searchers** (18.4.64)
'*Oh Well – Part 2*', **Fleetwood Mac** (11.10.69)
'*Don't Let Me Be Misunderstood*', **Joe Cocker** uncharted version of the Animals hit (6.2.65)
'*Stop Messin' Round*', **Fleetwood Mac** (album)
'*Shadoogie*', **Shadows** (album)
'*Daydream Believer*', uncharted recording by **Nick Berry** of the Monkees hit (25.11.67)

▲ *Landowner Raymond Walker (Peter Gilmore) wants an old lady's cottage – and his ally turns out to be closer to home than she imagined.*

Episode 6:
'The Frighteners'
Writer – Brian Finch
Director – Alan Grint

■ An elderly woman who lives in a charming but isolated cottage complains that she is being persecuted – there have been prowlers at night, nuisance phone calls and so on. Her cottage is wanted by a local landowner who is involved in a legal tussle with Greengrass regarding a footpath. The villain of the piece, however, turns out to be her son-in-law, anxious to get her into an old people's home and sell the cottage.

Meanwhile Ventress rescues a kitten from drowning, fails to find it a home and tries to keep it secretly at the police station. Blaketon finds out and orders Ventress to have the animal destroyed. He, Nick and Bellamy all refuse. Blaketon sets off to do the deed but is later discovered in his office with the kitten on his lap.

'*I Love My Dog*', **Cat Stevens** (22.10.66)
'*A Handful of Songs*', **Tommy Steele** (album)
'*Tutti Frutti*', **Swinging Blue Jeans** (album)
'*The Wanderer*', **Adam Faith** (album)
'*A Whiter Shade of Pale*', **Procol Harum** (25.5.67)
'*Sunny*', **Georgie Fame** (24.9.66)

Episode 7:
'Father's Day'
Writer – Brian Finch
Director – Terry Marcel

■ Nick arrests Blaketon's son Graham for mugging a suspected drug dealer. The boy claims that he did so to stop him pushing drugs to youngsters and that all the substances he took from him he destroyed. None the less Blaketon is horrified and insists the law must take its course – much to the fury of his ex-wife.

Nick tracks down a stash of counterfeit money. A rough-and-ready local widow is given a letter by Greengrass from her dead and estranged husband telling her the key to his safety deposit box is in the pocket of his best suit. But he was buried in his best suit. His family rob his grave, retrieve the deposit box and find it full of money – unfortunately all forged. They were set up.

'You're Driving Me Crazy', **Temperance Seven** (1.4.61)
'You Were Made For Me', **Freddie and the Dreamers** (9.11.63)
'Bad to Me', **Billy J. Kramer and the Dakotas** (3.8.63)
'Ferry Cross the Mersey', **Gerry and the Pacemakers** (19.12.64; rereleased and re-entered charts 20.5.89)
'Easy Going Me', **Adam Faith** (29.4.61)
'Goldfinger', **Shirley Bassey** (17.10.64)
'I Love How You Love Me', **Jimmy Crawford** (9.12.61)
'Daydream Believer', uncharted recording by **Nick Berry** of the Monkees hit (25.11.67)

▶ *Gold-digging widow Betty Such (Julie T. Wallace) gets a surprise when she digs too deep. . .*

117

Episode 8:
'Endangered Species'
Writer – Michael Russell
Director – Tim Dowd

■ An old lady is injured in a hit-and-run accident and her mentally handicapped son runs to the pub for help and luckily finds Nick and Kate there, out for the evening and playing darts.

There are badger baiters about and they are trying to involve the old lady and her son – he is a true countryman who knows the woodland around Aidensfield backwards. He also hates the idea of badger baiting. With the help of Greengrass, who is also opposed to killing badgers, Nick manages to trap those responsible.

Greengrass sells shares in his racehorse – unfortunately the shareholders discover that he has done so several times over.

| 'I Am the Walrus', **Beatles** (double EP, Magical Mystery Tour 16.12.67)
'The House that Jack Built', **Alan Price** (12.8.67)

Episode 9:
'An American in Aidensfield'
Writer – Peter Palliser
Director – Catherine Morshead

■ An American motor cyclist arrives in the village and is injured in an accident when he swerves to avoid some sheep. In need of a doctor, he finally arrives at the police house in search of Kate who, following Dr Ferrenby's death, has had to move her surgery there temporarily. Nick is in bed with flu but unfortunately gets little rest.

It transpires that the American is a draft dodger avoiding service in Vietnam and this infuriates a local man who is a veteran of Korea. He and some cronies pick a fight with the American.

But the American is not unpopular with all. Gina begins to fall in love with him and Greengrass is trying to make a quick buck as usual by selling him old English motor bikes which he acquired falsely, claiming he wanted to give them to his regimental museum.

| 'I Feel Free', **Cream** (7.1.67)
'Pamela Pamela', **Wayne Fontana** (17.12.66)
'Little Things', **Dave Berry** (27.3.65)
'Delta Lady', **Joe Cocker** (25.10.69)
'I Can See for Miles', **The Who** (21.10.67)
'With a Little Help from my Friends', **Joe Cocker** (12.10.68)

Episode 10:
'Bringing it all Back Home'
Writer – Michael Russell
Director – Bob Mahoney

■ Expanding careers causes problems between Nick and Kate. A new police inspector arrives and Nick will have a bigger beat. Kate is tempted to join a group practice in Whitby.

A charabanc outing is organized to hear Gina sing in a Whitby club. Bellamy gets involved in a fight in an amusement arcade and the day ends on a subdued note. Kate and Nick help a little girl try to find her father. Nick spots the man in trouble far out to sea and calls the lifeboat. But it is too late.

The Inland Revenue finally catch up with Greengrass who is in big trouble.

And Nick and Kate go on a picnic to talk things through. They agree that while their careers may draw them apart their marriage will remain as strong as ever.

▲ (Left) 'An American in Aidensfield': a concerned Gina tends injured American motorcyclist Bradley Lavelle (Charlie Cameron) and develops stronger feelings for him. (Right) 'Bringing it all Back Home': Whitby lifeboat goes to the rescue of a missing man.

❙ 'Big Spender', **Shirley Bassey** (21.10.67)
'Wheel of Fortune', **Kathy Kirby** (album)
'Father and Son', **Cat Stevens** (album)
'We Can Work It Out', sung on the show by **Tricia Penrose** and band, from the Beatles hit (11.12.65)

Series 4*

*Series 4 of *Heartbeat* runs for 16 episodes, of which only the first eight storylines were available before this book went to press.

Episode 1:
'Wild Thing'
Writer – Michael Russell
Director – Ken Horn

■ When sheep go missing from the hills of Aidensfield, Nick is called to investigate. Rustlers are suspected but the discovery of some badly mauled sheep suggest something more sinister. Whitby's new Inspector Crossley immediately initiates a search for a large wild animal, and Alfred becomes a suspect when he is found covered in white paint. Greengrass already has enough to worry about because the Inland Revenue are gradually catching up with him. However, he finds a novel way of meeting their demands.

Kate, meanwhile, is joining Dr James Radcliffe in a group practice in Whitby. Her first patient complains of flu symptoms, but Kate discovers he has a more mysterious illness.

Episode 2:
'Witch Hunt'
Writer – Brian Finch
Director – Catherine Morshead

■ The local kids in Aidensfield reckon Nancy Bellow is a witch. Nancy used to be a live-in help and companion to Amy Dewhurst, but when Amy died, the house was inherited by her relatives, Marjorie and Harry. Nancy herself received nothing in the will and had to move out of the house. She still cooks for Marjorie and Harry, so when they are taken to hospital with poisoning, Nancy is the obvious suspect. Nick checks the poison register and everyone's suspicions appear to be confirmed. The case prompts a battle for professional supremacy between Inspector Crossley and Sergeant Blaketon.

Episode 3:
'Midday Sun'
Writer – Jonathon Critchley
Director – Baz Taylor

■ Mike Halstood, an army officer discharged from service in Germany, is camping near Aidensfield with his family. To his son Jamie's distress, their dog has gone missing. Kate and Dr Radcliffe are treating Swaby, the local garage owner, in Ashfordly Hospital, where he is experiencing violent convulsions and a raging thirst. Panic then breaks out when rabies is diagnosed. Roadblocks are set up around the area but Jamie Halstood is still out looking for his dog.

There is a new police car for Ashfordly police station. Unfortunately, Ventress drives it first.

Episode 4:
'Turn of The Tide'
Writer – Johnny Byrne
Director – Tim Dowd

■ Nick and Ventress take a fishing trip together in Whitby, and also try their luck at poker. It may be Ventress's annual holiday, but Nick is undercover to investigate smuggling. They lodge with the Stirlings who run a sailing shop. When Nick spots a container being picked up at sea, he discovers that it is stuffed with counterfeit cash. He eventually persuades Jake Stirling to help him nail the perpetrators.

Jake's girlfriend discovers she is pregnant but Jake tells her she must have an abortion. She becomes desperate when Kate says she cannot help her as it is against the law. Back in Aidensfield, Greengrass makes the most of Nick's absence and enjoys a fine trade in venison.

Episode 5:
'Love Child'
Writer – Brian Finch
Director – Ken Horn

■ Nick disturbs a break-in at the Children's Department of Ashfordly Council Offices, but the burglar escapes with a bundle of blank postal orders and a file detailing an abortion. Meanwhile, Kate treats Sandie for a badly cut hand, and a toddler is abducted in Whitby.

Greengrass has discovered that pigeon-racing makes a fine day's recreation when combined with a few bottles of beer. He is enraged when nesting peregrine falcons kill one of his pigeons and Nick doesn't seem to think it is a

121

police matter. When two keen birdwatchers find that the falcons' eggs have been smashed, suspicion naturally falls on Greengrass.

Episode 6:
'Nice Girls Don't'
Writer – Jane Hollowood
Director – Baz Taylor

■ Whitby hosts a rugby match between the North Riding Police and the Harbourmen. At the cup presentation and general knees-up afterwards, Gina has a good time flirting with one of the harbourmen, and with Bellamy. As she drives home at the end of the evening, she realizes that she is being followed. Panicking, she stalls her car and is chased into the woods. But when the crime is reported, Inspector Murchison takes a very unsympathetic line and suggests that Gina is making it up. Fortunately, Nick is on the scene when the attacker strikes again, in Whitby.

Episode 7:
'Trouble in Mind'
Writer – Johnny Byrne
Director – Tim Dowd

■ A man called Parker reappears in Aidensfield unable to remember the last seven years of his life. When he left the village all those years ago, he abandoned his wife and child and disappeared after collecting his employer's payroll from the bank. Kate contacts his wife, Helen Parker, who reluctantly agrees to see her husband, and Nick investigates the disappearance of the payroll. Their enquiries take a new turn when another woman contacts Ashfordly police station claiming to be Parker's wife.

Greengrass goes to see 'Strangers on a Train' at the cinema and is very impressed by the plot, in which two strangers meet and arrange to carry out each other's crimes. There are therefore no motives to connect them to the crimes they commit. Later that evening, Greengrass is visited by a stranger with an interesting proposal.

Episode 8:
'Fair Game'
Writer – Veronica Henry
Director – Matthew Evans

■ Jack Temple-Richards arrives at the Aidensfield hunt in a terrible state. He is known as a heavy drinker but he doesn't normally seem any the worse for it. His wife, Susannah, is aghast to see him there in such a bad way but is unable to persuade him to go home. During the hunt, Jack falls from his horse when attempting a jump and dies. The pathologist's report notes that although Jack died of head injuries, there is also a high level of sleeping pills in his bloodstream – high enough to merit an inquiry.

Kate and Nick are called to the deathbed of Archie Cutter and are surprised to find Greengrass there as a mourner. He volunteers to look after Cutter's poultry and it is only when Nick is back at the police station that Blaketon informs him that Cutter was a notorious cock-fighter.

CAST LIST

PC Nick Rowan . . . . Nick Berry
Dr Kate Rowan . . . . Niamh Cusack
Sergeant Oscar Blaketon . . . . Derek Fowlds
Claude Jeremiah Greengrass . . . . Bill Maynard
Dr Alex Ferrenby . . . . Frank Middlemass
PC Alf Ventress . . . . William Simons
PC Phil Bellamy . . . . Mark Jordon
George Ward . . . . Stuart Golland
Gina Ward . . . . Tricia Penrose
Dr James Radcliffe . . . . Peter Firth
Inspector Crossley . . . . Russell Boulter
Inspector Murchison . . . . Karen Meagher
Christine Ferguson . . . . Julia Lane

GUEST APPEARANCES (IN ALPHABETICAL ORDER)

Series 1

Victoria Wainwright . . . . Jean Anderson
Maria Laszlo . . . . Eleanor Bron
Dick Radcliffe . . . . Paul Copley
Matthew Chapman . . . . James Cosmo
Penelope Stirling . . . . Annette Crosbie
Paul Melthorn . . . . John Duttine
Mary Radcliffe . . . . Lynn Farleigh
Harry Cottis . . . . Paul Greenwood
René Kirby . . . . Elizabeth Spriggs

Series 2

Sarah Collins . . . . Kitty Aldridge
Frank Milner . . . . Peter Barkworth
Susan Robinson . . . . Samantha Beckinsale

Clare Mercer . . . . Anna Calder Marshall
Nell Robinson . . . . Rachel Davies
Ken Marston . . . . Roland Gift
Reg Manston . . . . James Hazeldine
Marjorie Doubleday . . . . Anne Reid
Susan Rawlings . . . . Rachel Robertson
Amanda Young . . . . Dorothy Tutin

Series 3

Wilfred . . . . Duggie Brown
Jane Thompson . . . . Dora Bryan
Helen Lessor . . . . Anna Cropper
Florence Stockwell . . . . Rosalie Crutchley
Arcade Owner . . . . Freddie Davies
Tiny Weedon . . . . Freddie Garrity
Raymond Walker . . . . Peter Gilmore
Joan Forrester . . . . Sue Holderness
Jennifer Bradshaw . . . . Susan Jameson
Mr Parrish . . . . Freddie Jones
Martin Lessor . . . . Harold Innocent
Michael O'Leary . . . . TP McKenna
Eileen . . . . Anne Stallybrass
Victor Kellerman . . . . Clive Swift
Betty Such . . . . Julie T. Wallace

Series 4

Susannah Temple-Richards . . . . Jenny Agutter
Cedric Shanks . . . . Tim Healy
Nancy Bellow . . . . Phyllida Law